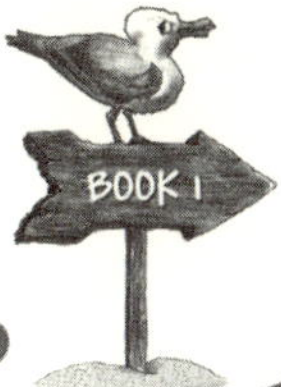

Turtle Town
The Inner Puka

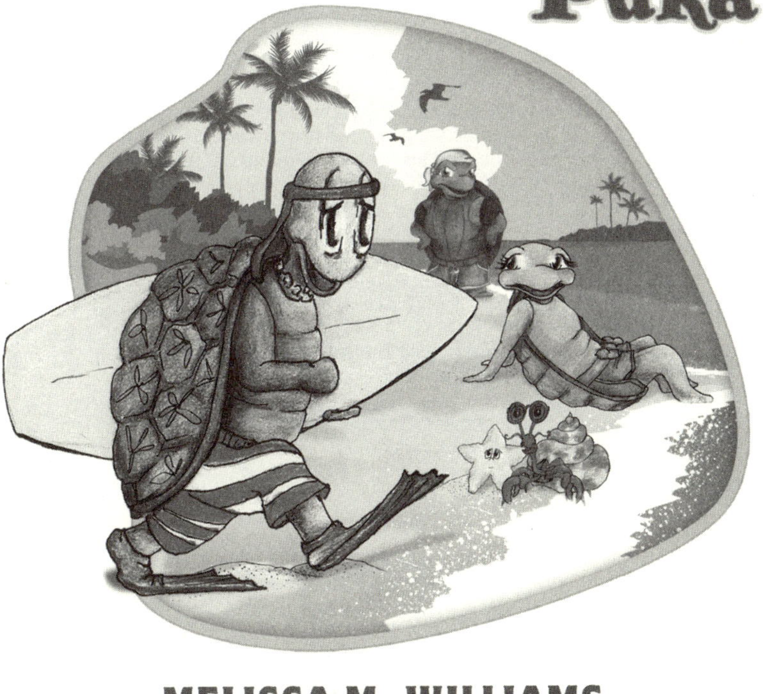

MELISSA M. WILLIAMS
Illustrated by Kelley Stengele

Copyright © 2011 by Melissa M. Williams

All rights reserved. Published by LongTale Publishing. No part of this book may be used or reproduced in any manner whatsoever without written permission from except in the case of brief quotation embodied in critical articles and reviews. Printed in the United States of America.

For information address Long Tale Publishing,
13039 Mossy Ridge Cove, Houston, TX 77041.

Sea Trek® and Trekker are copyrighted by Sub Sea Systems, Inc.
For more information about the Sea Trek helmet diving activity reflected by the "Trekker" character within this book visit
www.sea-trek.com

Library of Congress Control Number: 2011903890
ISBN 978-0-9818054-6-7 (Paperback)

JUVENILE FICTION / Animals / Turtles

Design by Monica Thomas for TLC Graphics
www.TLCGraphics.com

Interior text formatting by Sharon Wyatt
Illustrations by Kelley Stengele

In-house Editor: Bobby Ozuna
In-house Editor: Sharon Wyatt

www.turtletownbooks.com

*To the ones who have encouraged
creativity since my childhood, my parents.*

Table of Contents

Prelude 7

1. We Ain't in Texas Anymore Dude **15**
2. The Skater Chick Surfs Too **25**
3. Such a Tourist **41**
4. Snap Gets Dreadlocks **55**
5. First Time for Everything **73**
6. The 'Oia'i'o **93**
7. The Green Flash **107**
8. Good for Nothing Gill **125**
9. Snap Faces His Inner Cave **141**
10. The Shack **155**
11. Soul Surfing **165**
12. Morning Coffee Buzz **179**
13. Star Says His First Word **189**
14. No One is As They Seem **199**
15. Sara Shell **211**

About the Author 229
Acknowledgments 231
Special Acknowledgments 235

Prelude

Mother Nature hummed a soft tune, announcing the coming of a new season. All life within her swayed and swam, flowing in unison to her gentle melody. Snap Shell stood, eyes focused on the infinite sea before him—the life-source of all sea turtles. His entire world was the ocean, no land, only water as far as he could see. The waves were strong, rolling in every direction, crashing and folding over themselves without ever touching the land. Above him, lightning streaks flashed, and the sound of the thunder mimicked the roar of the sea.

Suddenly, his gaze was interrupted, as an ionic light shone down on the sea from the heavens, drawing his attention to one spot deep in the water. A giant sea turtle with glimmering designs on its shell emerged above the breaks and began moving in his direction. The sea turtle moved in, closer and closer, gliding across the water's surface. As fear came over Snap Shell he tried to move away, not knowing what to do, but his toes were stuck in the damp sand.

The sea turtle was very large, weighing more than a few hundred pounds, and its face had the look of one who was old and wise. As the turtle drew nearer to Snap, he was able to make out the vivid designs on its shell, glistening in the light and reflection of the sea. The symbols appeared to resemble an ancient day of the turtles, a time long diminished, along with the traditions that once bound the inner puka of one's life to a great species.

The sea turtle stood face-to-face with Snap Shell and looked into the young box shell turtle's eyes, as if it could see into his soul, and Snap could not look away. He was caught in a trance and remained motionless. The touch of the sea turtle's breath on Snap's face was like feeling the wind blowing over his shell the first time he ever saw the ocean.

The large sea turtle lifted its front flipper out of the water and reached slowly in Snap's direction. Snap looked down and realized the turtle was reaching for the necklace around his neck. Snap touched the necklace with both hands and the sea turtle nodded in approval. *But what does it mean?* Snap thought.

The sea turtle turned its head over its left shoulder, maintaining eye contact with Snap just long enough to redirect his attention. Snap Shell followed with his eyes to where the sea turtle was looking, and as he did the wind picked up, bringing with it the familiar fragrance of lavender and lilacs. Suddenly, there was another turtle far off in the water. Snap instantly recognized the scent, and a calming sense of comfort came over him. It was a feeling familiar to his youth, a feeling of security and protection. As Snap focused on the new turtle's image, his eyes grew wide in disbelief.

"Mom?" Snap asked. The word rippled across the water.

His mother smiled at him and began to speak, but Snap couldn't understand her. Her words were more like a vibration than sound, a vibration he could feel beneath his sandy feet. The more she

Prelude

spoke, the more it sounded like she was speaking with the waves as they rolled into the shore and crashed around him.

The lightning intensified, and Snap could see green flashes in the distance. Each flash carried an image of his past. He was collecting shells with his mother on the beach...painting his bedroom walls...picking out a surfboard on the seawall...driving away from a storm in his parents' car...

"Mom!" he yelled. His voice carried only as far as the wind would allow, and his words echoed in every direction. "How did you get here? What's happening?" Snap turned in desperation to the large sea turtle and said, "Who are you? Where are we? What's happening?" When he turned back to face his mother, he could only see the silhouette of a shell that a moment ago was the image of his mom.

What's happening? Snap thought. *Was she really here?* He began to panic and realized he was now standing in the middle of the ocean and an enormous wave was approaching. Above him the thunder cracked, and the waves began to grow stronger. Below him he could see the ocean bottom, miles and miles of deep canyons without an end. "I can't swim...I can't swim!" he cried. He turned to face the large sea turtle again and said, "Can you help me? I can't swim!"

The wave sucked all the water from below him, forming a hollow tube. Just as it came crashing down around him, it burst into millions of tiny shells that shined like crystals. They were puka shells like the ones his mother gave him that he wore around his neck. He closed his eyes and lifted his head as the waves of puka shells began to swallow him up. Just before he was completely engulfed, he felt a soft touch upon his shoulder and heard his mother calling his name. "Snap! Snap, wake up! It's time to go!"

Turtle Town: The Inner Puka

The voice became louder, almost as if in front of his face. "Snap...come on..." Snap tossed and grumbled, as he slowly opened one eye. Trying to regain focus, he opened his other eye and found himself looking directly into the peering eyes of a green iguana and his two dark nose holes. "Snap, I leave you for ten minutes and you manage to fall asleep on the only piece of furniture left in your house? Your dad said the moving truck is about ready to go," the iguana said.

Snap could feel and *smell* the iguana's hot breath. "Aww, dude! Back up. Have you been eating onions or something?" Snap groaned, pushing his best friend away.

"I knew there were onions on that veggie burger!" Iggy held his hand in front of his mouth to check out his breath, quivering at the stench. "Oh, gosh, that smells awful."

"Ya think dude?" Snap asked, yawning and rubbing his eyes. "I think I was having a dream."

"Yeah, you were!" Iggy laughed. "By the way, who's Wrinklebutt, anyway?" the iguana asked. "And do you have a mint?"

"Wrinkle what? What are you talking about?" Snap still appeared dazed and tried to focus on his friend.

"I don't know. You were the one who kept saying it," Iggy told him.

Snap scratched the top of his head and adjusted his necklace. "Wrinklebutt? That's just weird dude." He shrugged and rolled over on the sofa, turning the back of his shell toward the green iguana.

The movers walked inside and lifted up the couch Snap was on. Snap felt himself being lifted off the ground, disrupting his sense of balance, and he fell to the floor.

"Seriously dudes? Didn't you see me on the couch?"

The movers didn't respond to Snap's question as they took the last piece of furniture out the door.

Prelude

Snap rolled over and sat on the ground for a moment, trying to remember his dream, but the only thing he could recall was the feeling of being swallowed by the ocean and the image of his mother. *Mom!* He thought. Snap hurried off the floor and ran to his bedroom, remembering the last few things he wanted to personally carry out of the house before they left.

"Hey, where are you going?" Iggy followed his buddy.

The box shell turtle was lost in deep thought as he moved through the empty house. He figured it was normal to dream about the ocean. The anticipation of living by the beach again was all he thought about. Ever since his father broke the news to him, his mind had been fixed on only one thing—California. There he would find real waves, real surfing, and live in one of the most highly populated turtle societies in the country.

He walked through his empty bedroom into the bathroom to collect the last remaining item on the counter. Snap picked up a frame, which held a picture of his mom. He heard the flopping and tapping sound of his best friend's toenails coming up behind him. "Hey Iggy, do you mind grabbing that last box outside my door?" Snap asked, hoping for a moment to himself.

"The one with the posters in it?" Iggy yelled.

Snap smiled. "Yeah dude, the one with surf posters in it."

Snap stared at the picture of his mother for a moment then closed his eyes, replaying the image of his mom from his dream in his head. He often worried that he might forget her as he got older. He worried that his memories would become nothing more than stories relayed by his father, intermeshed with images from pictures he collected in his room and especially the one he held in his hand. He opened his eyes and took one long, last look in the mirror and stuffed the frame into his over-packed shell. Returning to his bedroom, he found his best friend rummaging through the box he was supposed to be moving.

"Man, why are you unpacking my box?" Snap hovered over the iguana, who was busy digging through the interesting items. Inside were books, surf magazines and maps of the various beaches in California.

His best friend sighed, then said, "You're going to love California, Snap," as he rolled up a poster of the great Shell Shlater surfing a huge wave at Pipeline in Hawaii. "I just can't wait 'til I can come and visit."

Snap watched, as his best friend tried to conceal a lone tear from rolling down his cheek. "Come on dude, don't cry. We'll see each other soon, right?" Snap tried to make Iggy feel better as he fought back a sudden tear of his own. "I'll email you when I get there. First thing. I promise!"

"Promise?" Iggy asked, turning to face his friend.

"Totally dude."

"And I want pictures too. And some seashells would be nice. Oh, and..."

Iggy was interrupted by Mr. Shell, who was calling for his son at the front door. "Snap, are you ready?"

"Coming Pops!" Snap tried not to sound too excited to leave in front of his best friend. He knew he would miss Iggy most of all.

The two walked to the front door together. "Bye, man." Snap held out his arm, and the two reptiles hugged. In a moment of silence, Snap thought about all the good times he had with Iggy, the memories they made together over the past year. He thought of their days together in Mrs. Buff's class, playing baseball in his backyard, and the lake trip they took together where Iggy helped him learn to swim.

Prelude

"You going to let go dude?" Snap joked. "You're crushing my shell."

"Oh, sorry, you can go." Iggy stepped back so Snap could make his way outside.

The last box was carefully loaded in the moving truck, and Snap wrestled his way to get his overstuffed shell into the seat next to his father, ready for the long road-trip ahead.

Mr. Shell patted him on the leg before pulling out of the driveway. "Ready, son?"

Snap nodded as he looked through his side mirror at Iggy waving good-bye from the vacant front porch. Behind him, Snap would leave the world that had become his home, the extended family of friends who welcomed him into their hearts and one true friend—a green iguana named Iggy.

We Ain't In Texas Anymore, Dude!

"Welcome to *Turtle Town Surf School*," Snap Shell stood in front of the sign mounted across an old balsa wood surfboard buried deep in the sand along the boardwalk. "Duuude," he said to himself as he breathed in the fresh, salty air. He couldn't believe he was actually in California, standing before the object of his affection. Snap ran his hand along the smooth wood, admiring the perfect shaping of the antique surfboard. The box shell turtle had waited years to be back at the beach for this very moment, and what better place to be for surfing than on the West Coast.

"You surf, sonny?" A voice echoed from behind him.

Snap jumped and immediately removed his hand from the board. "Hey!" He turned, expecting to shake a flipper, or at the very least see a sea turtle. Instead, to his surprise, he found himself standing face-to-face with a strange looking lizard wearing some sort of bubble contraption on his head. He looked like something from a science-fiction movie.

Duuude? What in the world? Snap thought.

"What's your name, sonny?" the lizard asked. As he spoke, fog formed and filled the glass helmet to the point Snap could barely see his face. The lizard let out a quick shot of air, and the fog disappeared instantly. *Phfff.*

"Snap...Snap Shell," he said with a look of confusion.

"Well Snap Snap Shell, I'm Trekker, but call me Trek for short." *Phfff.*

"It's just one Snap."

"One Snap for short coming up." *Phfff.* "Are you going in or just window-shopping, One Snap?" *Phfff.*

"Huh?"

"Well, do you surf?" Trek asked. *Phfff.*

"Well, yeah, dude...I, um...of course I do...but..."

"But what? All turtles surf in Turtle Town." *Phfff.*

"Maybe sea turtles," Snap said. "But I'm not exactly a...um...you know?" Snap tilted his head and directed Trekker's attention toward his un-webbed feet. "A *sea* turtle."

"Hmm," Trekker started, tapping a long finger on the glass of his helmet. "Oh well, come on, it can't hurt to try. All you need is a surfboard, which I have plenty of for sale." *Phfff.*

Snap worked to conceal his grin, realizing now the reason why Trekker made the weird sound at the end of every sentence. He had to blow out air in order to clear the condensation formed by his lizard breath. Each time he talked, his face disappeared behind a cloud of wetness stuck to the glass casing and then, like magic, the fog disappeared again. He wanted to ask what it was for and why he hadn't taken it off yet but was afraid that maybe the lizard had some kind of medical issue, or maybe it was some kind of California germ proof device, so he refrained.

"So?" Trekker started again. *Phfff.*

We Ain't in Texas Anymore, Dude!

Snap did have a surfboard that he brought with him from Texas, although, up to this point in his life, he never really used it. His mother promised to teach him years ago, before she died, and his father wasn't really one for getting in the ocean at all, unless it was directly related to his work.

"Dude, I've always wanted to surf in California, but I would have to ask my dad first." Snap knew there would be a 50/50 chance that his dad would agree and say yes.

"Your dad?" *Phfff.* "You have to ask your dad for permission to surf?" *Phfff.*

"No," Snap said matter-of-factly. "I mean, it's cool and all dude." Snap tried to come up with an excuse. "I just gotta get my surfboard out. We just moved here, and it's packed away and all."

"It's not like you have to pay tuition or anything," Trekker said, clearly not listening to Snap's prior response. "The Turtle Board funds a bunch of programs for us. Like underwater adventures, snorkeling, scuba diving and summer school surfing, of course." *Phfff.* Trekker handed Snap a pamphlet with all of the activities

funded by the Turtle Board and an old map of the California beaches.

"It's a great way to make friends, if you give it a try." *Phfff.*

Snap nodded while opening up the crinkled old map. "Okay, Trek. I'll be back tomorrow morning." Surf school would be a perfect way to meet some new turtles, and maybe a few lizards for that matter.

Trekker tilted his helmet in a nod and waved goodbye.

Snap folded up his map and pamphlet and stuffed them into the back of his shell, while looking around. "Hmm. What to do next?" He walked down a large set of wooden stairs to get a better look at the beach and do some animal watching. The beach was full of all kinds of sea turtles. Loggerheads, Leatherbacks, Greens, Olive Ridleys and Hawksbills were hanging out on the beach, and of course, surfing. Snap recognized each of the different breeds of his native turtles making up the population of Cardiff Beach. It made sense why Southern California was called Turtle Town, not to mention, all of the turtles looked noticeably different on the West Coast. Not only were the sea turtles much bigger than the box shell turtles back home, but they all walked on only their two hind legs, unlike Snap and his father who walked on their hands and feet.

"Wow!" he said, fascinated to see it in real life. "How do they do it?" he said out loud as a sea gull perched beside him on a rock. All of the sea turtles were balancing on just their two back flippers. He had only seen it on TV and Turtle Tube.

"Squawk. Squawkedy-squawk. Squawk-squawk." A seagull called over Snap's shoulder.

"Pardon?" Snap asked, as if he spoke seagull.

"Squawk!"

We Ain't in Texas Anymore, Dude!

What an obnoxious language, Snap thought to himself. He moved a few inches over, away from the annoying bird to continue with his inspection of the surrounding turtles, and as he did, the seagull moved a few inches closer.

"Seriously dude? Can I help you?" Snap shooed the seagull away.

The seagull leaned in toward Snap and started licking his chops.

"Dude, back up. What's your deal?"

The seagull snapped at Snap's throat, which caused him to defensively grab his puka shell necklace hanging from his neck.

"Get out of here!" Snap jumped up and the seagull flew off.

"Awkward!" As Snap turned toward the sidewalk, he caught a faint glimpse of a bright pink blur on a skateboard coming straight for him. Before he could react, it plowed right into him and a little turtle went flying over his head and landed hard on the other side of the sidewalk, directly on her feet. "Argh!"

Afraid she might be hurt, Snap quickly rolled over on the ground. "Are you okay?" Snap shouted, scrambling to pick up her skateboard.

"Dude! You make a totally dangerous jump!" The turtle checked to make sure all sides of her pink board skirt were down and grabbed her skateboard from Snap's hand.

"Sorry about that," he blushed. Snap was a bit surprised to see the pretty little turtle standing in front of him, and with a skateboard.

"No worries, man!" She threw her skateboard down and jumped back on.

"Umm. Thanks. I'm really happy...I mean, sorry." Snap stood there, tongue-tied. He shook his head, agitated at his own lack of a cool response. "I'm really happy? Seriously?" He rolled his eyes.

By this time, the seagull had reappeared and was perched on the stairwell over his shoulder. It let out a loud squawk and Snap said, "I hear ya, man," to the seagull as he watched the turtle skate down the boardwalk. "Now that is the cutest skateboarding surfer chick turtle I've ever seen," he told the seagull, forgetting how annoying the bird had been a few minutes ago.

One thing became instantly apparent to the box shell turtle. If he didn't find a way to fit in with the turtles in Turtle Town, they may call him a poser, or even worse, a wanna-be. He had but one option, learn how to surf, and he had to learn quickly! Living in a place like California, Snap had no other choice.

Snap made the long walk up the hill to his house and noticed his dad outside, cleaning off the balcony with a water hose. Mr. Shell was always doing something, which usually consisted of cleaning, working, or talking about his work as a marine biologist. Snap couldn't believe that he had actually made it three whole days in the moving truck with his father on their drive from Texas to California. Twenty-two hours on the highway, listening to hours upon hours of talk radio, audio books about ocean life and recordings of whale sounds was enough to make Snap want to rip the shell off his back from sheer boredom.

As Snap watched his dad scrub the dirt off the lawn furniture, he remembered the one and only cool part about their road trip when they stopped at the historic Grand Canyon and along the New Mexican desert to visit an old buddy of Snap's father, a dusty desert tortoise. Although Snap gave the impression he was *too cool* to partake in their silly military stories as they recollected their *glory days* of service across oceans far and wide, he still listened. It was good for Snap to see his father smile again. He even laughed

We Ain't in Texas Anymore, Dude!

to himself as he heard of his father's crazy adventures before he met Snap's mom, of course. It was a huge contrast between the boring box shell turtle he now watched watering the balcony and cleaning the lawn furniture.

Snap shook his head while taking a moment to catch his breath as he hopped up one more flight of stairs outside the balcony. "Hey Pops, it's looking good out here." Snap sat down, hoping his dad was in a good mood to listen to his surf school proposal.

"Thanks son. I think we need to add a few more plants out here. What do you think? Just needs a little more greenery." Mr. Shell smiled, agreed with himself, and continued to water the balcony without waiting on his son's reply.

Snap got straight to the point, "I met a new friend today. He told me about the surf school. It starts tomorrow." Snap gritted his teeth as he waited again.

"Oh?" his father said, scratching off some moss that started to grow on one of the lawn chairs. When it didn't come off, he scratched his head, leaving a piece of the moss on the crown of his head.

Snap watched his father and laughed. It looked like he had grown a sprout of hair on his bald head. "Uh, Pops? Uh, you have," he started, pointing to his father's head. "Moss."

Mr. Shell nodded. "Yeah son, it won't come off," he said and continued to spray down the chair. "Once this stuff starts growing, it's tough to wipe clean."

Snap ignored him, realizing his father didn't understand what he was saying. "So, what do you think?" he continued.

"Think about what son?"

"Surf school?"

"What about surf school?" his father asked.

"I was thinking about taking some lessons. At the surf school I just told you about. It will be a great way to meet new animals, Pops. Make new friends, you know?"

"Surf school, huh?" Mr. Shell turned off the water and walked inside as he motioned for his son to follow. "Shouldn't you be getting ready for *real* school, son?"

"Cardiff Elementary doesn't start for at least another month, Pops!" Snap followed Mr. Shell into the house and continued toward the study. Mr. Shell had brought with him another piece of the moss he found stuck under his nail and sat down in his chair. He immediately placed the moss under his prized possession—his microscope. Although Mr. Shell spent all day studying the beach, its inhabitants, plants, and organisms, he usually didn't pay too much attention to ocean activities.

"You know surfing is very dangerous," his father said. He was busy elevating and lowering the microscope to get a closer look at the moss.

"That's why I should take lessons."

Mr. Shell pulled his eye away from the microscope and let out a heavy sigh. He knew how much the ocean meant to his son. Ever since the first day they settled on Galveston Beach in Texas, his son had a passion for the waves and the surf life. He knew his son couldn't swim, but thanks to Snap's friend Iggy, and a pair of blue flippers, he learned how. Mr. Shell figured there was no way for his son to avoid surfing, having moved to one of the most popular surf towns in the country. "As long as this doesn't effect your grades son, I suppose it's okay."

"Really?" Snap smiled and hugged his father, nearly knocking over the microscope. "It won't Pops! I promise!" Snap ran to his room to get his surfboard and gear ready for his first day at surf school. He spent the rest of the night pinning up surf posters on his bedroom walls and watching videos about surfing on Turtle Tube. He even pretended to surf from the mattress on his bed while also *attempting* to hold himself up on his hind legs. Snap spent his entire life dreaming of the day he would surf the real ocean, and finally that dream was about to come true.

CHAPTER 2
The Skater Chick Surfs Too

The next day Snap walked to the surf school with his long-board tied to the top of his shell and his flippers hidden inside of it. Once he reached the sign in front of the school, he looked for the lizard in the bubble helmet, hoping that he would be there for some moral support. Snap felt uneasy walking in on his hands and feet, like some prehistoric turtle who hadn't learned how to eat with a fork and knife yet. He tried to remain confident and not let the fact that all the other turtles walked on their hind legs get to him. He would probably have bigger obstacles in the ocean.

"Snap Snap!" Trekker screamed from across the way.

Snap was happy to see him. "It's only *one* Snap," he said.

Phfff. "What was that?" the lizard asked.

Nothing, Snap thought.

"So glad you made it." *Phfff.* "I want to introduce you to your surf instructor, Timmy Turtle."

Snap fumbled to balance the long-board on his back while looking up at the very strong turtle standing over him. Timmy was a large Green Sea Turtle with a firm chiseled jaw and a muscular body that gave the impression he had been riding the waves of Turtle Town for years. "Welcome, brah! Glad to have a tortoise join the team."

"Ah, thanks man," Snap said from behind his surfboard.

"You'll be Tula's partner," Timmy said, as he pointed toward a sea turtle down by the shore.

Snap tried to focus past his long-board that was obstructing his vision as it pressed down on his head.

"Over here," the sea turtle said, waving him over to join her.

"Oh, great!" Snap mumbled under his breath when he spotted his surf partner's bright pink board skirt. It was the cute little skater chick turtle from yesterday.

Snap waddled over as fast as his heavy shell would let him with his board dragging in the sand behind him. "I think you and I are..." Snap started.

The turtle interrupted him before he could finish. "Hey, I'm Tula." She smiled at him and batted her lashes.

The Skater Chick Surfs Too

She was an Olive Ridley, and she made an impression on Snap Shell rather quickly. That same feeling of not knowing what to do or say came back over him as he fumbled for his words. "Um. Hey. I'm Snap," he gulped, still trying to play it cool. "Sorry about yesterday," he said, apologizing for their collision. Snap looked down and untied the rope around his shell holding his board.

Tula didn't seem to remember. "Nice puka shells," she said, smiling.

Snap looked up quickly and grabbed his necklace. "Thanks, it was a gift."

"You're not from around here, huh?" she questioned.

"What gave it away?"

"Dude, you're a box shell. Box shell turtles don't live in Cali. Well, on the beach that is, they're more of the inland city type, you know?"

Snap laughed when she called him dude. It was such a habit for him to call everyone dude, that hearing it from another turtle, especially a girl, made him feel weird. All he could say was, "Dude." He squinted, wishing again that he had said something more interesting.

"So, how did you get here anyway?" Tula asked while playing with a puka shell bracelet that hung around her wrist.

Snap tried to be witty, to help conceal his awkwardness. "It took some time, but I swam across the Pacific Ocean." He was the only one who laughed.

"Very funny, smarty pants." She knew box shell turtles couldn't swim, and rarely would they come down to the beach.

"My dad and I drove," Snap admitted, a bit flustered.

Tula giggled at Snap's answer. "So how are you going to surf?" She motioned toward Snap's un-webbed feet.

Snap reached into his shell and pulled out a pair of blue flippers. "With these," he said.

Tula smiled as she watched Snap put on his flippers, and Snap could feel her eyes peering down at his feet.

The two of them were interrupted by Trekker, as he started class. "Good morning, surfers!" *Phfff.*

Thank you, Snap thought as he and Tula joined the group of sea turtles to hear what Trekker had to say.

The lizard gave an introduction to the group, telling the history of the surf school between quick shots of air to clear his helmet. *Phfff.* "Turtle Town Surf School started back in the 1990s by my father, Sir Trek," he said. He went on to describe the other Turtle Town Surf School locations across the ocean.

"What's up with the bubble helmet thing?" Snap asked Tula.

Tula laughed. "It's called the Sea Trek Helmet. He and his dad invented that helmet for this company here in Cali called Sub Sea Systems. His dad named it after him and his son. Trek also runs the surf shop next door. *And* he's one of the most respected board shapers here in Southern California."

"What does it do?"

"The helmet?"

"Yeah," Snap said.

"It's for all the animals in California who love the ocean but can't breathe underwater. Pretty much everyone in Cali knows Trek because of his family business," Tula explained.

Trekker turned the stage over to Timmy. "Dudes and Dudettes!"

"Nicccce!" Tula hissed in excitement. "I'm so stoked that Timmy's back to teach us this year."

"Why?" Snap questioned.

The Skater Chick Surfs Too

"He's totally legit. Timmy knows so many pros. Shell Shlatter, Surfdog..." She paused and raised a brow, "He's been gone all year chasing the perfect wave."

"No way! Shell Shlatter?" Snap grew interested in Timmy when he heard this particular bit of information. He couldn't believe how *real* everything seemed to him. He pictured the great Shell Shlatter from his magazines. He knew if Timmy knew Shell, he definitely had some serious surfing skills.

Timmy walked up to Snap and peered down at his blue flippers. "Those are some gnarly webs you got there. Do they actually work?" Before Snap had a chance to answer, he was interrupted by a high-pitched French accent coming from behind his new surf instructor.

"Sorry we're late, Timmy," the foreign voice stated. "Star insisted on cleaning my shell again." A peculiar looking hermit crab, wearing goggles, crept up to Timmy's side. He had a starfish stuck to his back, who appeared to be nibbling away at his shell.

Timmy pretended not to hear the crab's apology and started to put some *Tur-tle Wax* on Snap's shiny board. "There you go, man. You would have been slipping all over the place on that brand new board of yours."

Some of the students laughed.

"Thanks, bro, I've had it for a few years, just haven't had a chance to use it." Snap made a mental note to run down to the surf shop to pick up some more wax for his ex-wall decoration he'd brought from Texas. Snap glanced over at the hermit crab and starfish. The starfish had managed to release himself from his ride, or possibly lunch, and was now jumping up and down with what looked to be a coffee cup.

Turtle Town: The Inner Puka

"Is he drinking...?" Snap started.

Tula laughed and patted Snap Shell on the back. "I'll tell you about them later."

"And I thought crabs could see under water?" Snap said, referring to the goggles on the hermit crab's beady eyes.

"They're prescription," Tula whispered, signaling for Snap to be quiet with one finger.

"Oh." Snap scratched his head. *I've seen it all now,* he thought.

Timmy continued, "See these crustaceans, these are my assistants. Herbert..."

"*Bonjour,*" the crab bowed to the audience, his claws folded behind his back in a sort of mock curtsy.

"...and Star," Timmy continued. The starfish said nothing and hopped on and off Herbert's back ten or more times during his introduction. Timmy stared at Star and shook his head. "If you need these guys for help," Timmy paused to look down at the pair who seemed to be in an argument over whether Star should stay or remove himself from Herbert's back, "Well, good luck with that."

"I am at your service," the hermit crab said, walking around the crowd of students, introducing himself to each one individually. He handed each student a business card. "Here you are, *monsieur.*" Herbert handed Snap his card.

"Um, thanks?" Snap shook his claw.

The card had a picture of Herbert's face, or actually mostly his eye balls, with the line: *Assistant with a Star at your service!*

"Okay, enough of that. Back to business everyone!" Timmy shouted. "It's time to review the basics." Timmy spent the first twenty minutes going over rip currents, swells, barrels, and the importance of not pearling. Timmy made a gesture toward Snap and said, "Pearling is basically the result of being too far up on your board so that the nose of your board goes under water. *Not a good thing.*"

The class ended with a quick demonstration of Timmy hopping up on his board while it was still in the sand. Before he turned the students over to practice, he moved in closer to Snap to address a slight dilemma and potential problem. "Brah," Timmy said. "We're going to have to teach you some balancing tricks before you'll be any good on a board." He made a gesture to Snap's upright posture and said, "You're in California now, dude. No one here walks on their hands. That's more of a southern thing, I guess."

Tula noticed the discouraged look on her new friend's face and when Timmy turned around to other students, she whispered, "Don't worry, we'll practice, dude."

Snap Shell smiled and returned a *dude* in gratitude.

Timmy turned back to Snap, "But hey, I can tell you've got some spunk. No worries. You'll be up in no time, walking *and* surfing like the rest of us."

Snap knew he had so much to work on and practice before the next class, so he paid close attention to his new instructor, just trying to soak it all in. Herbert took on his duty as assistant and dusted off the sand on each turtle's board every time they tried hopping up on their own. Once each turtle had a turn, Timmy gave a few more pointers and handed everyone a sheet of paper, that was until Herbert insisted that passing out any type of paperwork was his job.

Snap looked down at the paper of surf-vocabulary words. He hadn't expected homework at surf school, but this was different. This was fun. *Awesome,* Snap thought.

"I want you to make sure you know what all of these mean by tomorrow. If you don't have a surf dictionary, you can always go look at the one I keep at the surf shop.

Later dudes!" With that, Timmy disappeared, signing a few autographs for some of the young turtles on the beach and posing for pictures along the way.

"Timmy actually wrote that dictionary," Tula said, folding her homework. Most of Snap's classmates grabbed their boards and headed down to the water, but Tula stayed behind with Snap.

"So, Boxy, want to go grab a snow cone?" she asked.

"Boxy?"

"Just joking. Anyway, I'm going to the snow cone stand if you want to come."

"Really?" Snap's eyes widened.

"Follow me." Tula grabbed her board and walked a few feet ahead of Snap, while he tried to push his board with the top of his head.

"There has got to be a better way to do this, right?" Snap yelled to Tula.

"Oh, geez." She smiled and grabbed his board with both of her hands. "This is exactly why we walk on two feet in Cali. How else are you going to carry your board? And to be honest, you look ridiculous." Tula patted Snap on the head.

"Ya wanna give me a hand then?" Snap asked.

Tula dropped Snap's board and held out both of her hand flippers in front of him and moved in relatively close. Snap stared with a blank, scared look on his face, his eyes focused on her open flippers.

"What? Come on already. I'm not asking you to dance. I'm going to teach you how to walk." Tula giggled, grabbed Snap's hands and managed to push him halfway up. "Come on man, you're going to have to use some ab-muscles here and help me out," she said as she pushed against his undershell.

Snap couldn't believe how strong she was for such a tiny thing. Once the box shell was completely vertical, Tula took hold of his

The Skater Chick Surfs Too

hands again and tried to help him relax, but before she could warn him, Snap fell backward taking her with him. Snap landed on the backside of his shell, belly up, with Tula now lying on top of him. She scrambled to get off him when her cheek fell onto Snap's face and their eyes met for a brief moment. Snap blushed and look away. Tula wrestled to get back on her feet and dusted the sand off her face. She peered over at Snap, trying to figure out a better way to get him up.

"Um, help?" Snap groaned. "I don't want to stay like this too long, ya know? Turtles do die on their backs."

"Calm down, calm down," Tula said. "I happen to be a turtle myself, and I doubt anyone's going to leave a helpless box turtle lying on his back, dude." Tula stuffed her hand into her shell, hoping to find something to use, and as she did, a shadow started to form across Snap. The shadow grew bigger and bigger and soon covered the radius around herself and the box shell turtle.

"Well, well. Look what we have here."

Tula instantly recognized the deep voice and turned around to defend her new friend. "Leave him alone Lucas," she said to the large Leatherback turtle.

When Snap lifted his head to check out their company, he couldn't tell if Tula was talking to a kid or a teenager. Lucas was by far the biggest turtle Snap had seen on the beach, and by no means was he chubby. He looked like a body builder turtle or maybe even a wrestler turtle. Lucas planted his shiny yellow *Tortuga* surfboard firmly into the sand and casually stood next to it. Snap knew he was good if he had a *Tortuga* short board. Pros use those thrusters for competing.

"You can't be serious, Tu-Tu. You think you're going to get that B.T. off his back?" Lucas laughed, kicking sand over Snap's shell.

"B.T.?" Snap questioned under his breath.

"What is a box turtle doing on the beach anyway?" Lucas said, laughing.

"Well," Tula huffed, working again to help Snap get upright. "He's learning how to surf. Not that it's any of your business."

"Ha! Get off the beach. No way!" Lucas said.

"Go back to your nitwits and bench press some stones or something. We've got this," Tula retorted.

Snap grinned at her comeback. She was quite a firecracker. Suddenly, Snap could hear motors in the distance over their arguing. The sound was getting louder and closer. It almost sounded like a herd of lawnmowers, but there was obviously no grass in sight.

"Tula, do you hear that?" Snap spoke up.

Tula was still too busy arguing with Lucas that she didn't notice, or maybe she just didn't care that a group of turtles on mopeds started to surround them on the beach.

"Well, great. You had to call your creatons over here, too?"

"Creatons?" Lucas asked.

The Skater Chick Surfs Too

"Your cronies. Your silly little followers," Tula said with her flippers on her hip shell. "Just leave us alone, Lucas!"

"Oh, so you *want* to be *alone*?"

"You're so immature."

Lucas' buddies started to laugh and revved the motors to their mopeds. Their wheels kicked sand in Snap's eyes and face, almost covering him. This was not what Snap had pictured when he dreamt of living on the West Coast. One Leatherback in a leather jacket popped a wheelie, which encouraged all of the others to do the same. Before Snap knew it, they were surrounded by the sound of mopeds, shouts and laughter and of course, more sand. He began to freak out, not sure what to do.

The entire spectacle lasted a few moments before it was abruptly stopped by the sound of an extremely loud conch shell being blown in the wind. The sound hummed across the entire beach. The seagulls left their rocks, crabs dug holes to bury themselves in the sand, and all the turtles on the beach held their hands over their ears, even Lucas.

The Leatherbacks backed away from Snap as soon as they saw Timmy Turtle making his way toward them with the trusty hermit crab and starfish by his side.

"You think you can skip class and mess with my students on top of that?" Timmy yelled, his face only inches away from Lucas.

Lucas put his head down, and in the process, dropped his board to the sand. "Sorry Tim, we're just having some fun with the new guy, that's all." Lucas took off his bandana to show some respect to Timmy and when he did, the other members of his group did the same.

"Fun? I don't see anyone laughing but the group of you," Timmy said. "Well, if I catch you messing with him again, you're going to be disqualified from Surf Barrel 39 this year!" He looked around to address the rest of the bale of turtles and said, "And that goes for the rest of you who plan on competing."

Snap watched as Tula's eyes grew wide in disbelief at Timmy's words.

"Alright, alright, show's over." Timmy motioned for everyone to leave.

Lucas shook his head and walked away with the rest of the Leatherbacks slowly riding behind him. A nosey flock of sea gulls that had perched to watch for sheer entertainment, followed the bale of turtles off the beach, squawking and screeching at each other.

"See you tomorrow Lucas," Timmy said. "And try not to be late for class."

Timmy looked over at Snap Shell. "Snap Snap, you okay, dude?"

Tula reminded Timmy it was only one Snap.

"Oh, right. Trek must have written it down wrong," Timmy sighed.

Snap started to sink deeper into the wet sand. "Yeah, I'm fine."

"We were trying to balance him on two feet, Timmy," Tula said.

"Hmm. I see that." Timmy crinkled his brow and grabbed Snap's hands, pulling him out of the sand trap. He let go just in time so both of Snap's hands would catch him.

Timmy and Tula studied Snap for a moment, trying to determine the best way to help him. Just then, the hermit crab and starfish arrived back on the scene with what looked to be a miniature shovel and a bucket the size of a walnut. "May I make a suggestion?" Herbert asked while digging tiny holes of sand away from Snap's shell. Star was sipping some coffee in a fancy to-go cup and occasionally dipping a portion of Herbert's shell into his cup before he drank from it.

The Skater Chick Surfs Too

"What is it, Herb?" Timmy asked, almost irritated. "And must you use that French accent?"

"*Oui, oui.* But of course, sir," Herbert stated. With a bow, he finished with, "I am French after all."

Star winked and shook his head in disagreement behind him.

Tula asked Herbert what advice he might have to help the situation.

"Where did your flippers go, *Monsieur* Snap Shell?"

"They're in my shell." Snap started fishing around for his flippers.

Timmy looked at Herbert as though he was going to compliment his advice but didn't. "Well put those puppies on so you can balance."

"Why didn't I think of that?" Tula threw up her hands. "Of course! Your flippers will help you stay up!"

After Snap put on his flippers, the trio tried once more to help the box shell balance himself and more importantly, walk. This time Snap stood balanced so perfectly on his flippers that he even surprised himself. He lifted one foot out of the muddy sand, making a squishy sound and plopped it out in front of him with his other flipper following.

"Well, problem solved. Looks like you won't be taking those off for a while." Timmy smiled while Tula and Star clapped.

"*Bravo! Bravo!*" Herbert said.

"Wait, isn't that Italian?" Tula asked.

Herbert folded his claws over his body and lifted his nose in the air. "Oh, aren't we the linguist?"

Snap started to walk faster and faster until he was running circles in the sand.

"Way to go, Boxy!" Tula jumped up and down.

Herbert joined in on the excitement and started sprinting from side to side, dodging Snap's flippers.

"Well, little turtles, I'm out. Time to get some sleep. Expecting a big swell at dawn." Timmy said as he waved good-bye from over his shoulder.

"Where you surfin'?" Tula asked.

"At the point. I'm dawn patrolling it tomorrow!"

"Have a good ride!" Snap yelled.

Timmy turned quickly and gave Snap a thumbs up.

"So, race you to the snow cone stand?" Snap reminded Tula of their plans.

"You bet!" Tula said, and the pair darted up the beach, this time with Snap holding his surfboard in both hands.

The two turtles bought snow cones from an old walrus behind the counter and then found a spot to sit and talk together on the beach.

"So, who was that creep, anyway?" Snap asked in regards to the biker turtle.

"That was Lucas." Tula sighed, "He's what you would call an arrogant *creaton*."

"Yeah, he did seem pretty full of himself, if you ask me."

"Ya think! I mean, he *is* the best kid surfer in Southern California and all, but the problem is, he *knows it*. He wins Surf Barrel every year in Trestles."

"Is he supposed to be in our surf class or something?"

"Yeah, but I'm sure he'll skip half of them like always. He thinks he's too good for surf school." Tula got up to throw away her empty cone and offered to take Snap's. She threw both away in a *paper only* bin. "Well, I should go. See you tomorrow, Boxy," she said and left Snap to walk uphill with his flippers and board by himself.

"Okay then, see you tomorrow." Snap got up, preparing himself for the long hike home as Tula skipped down the boardwalk. He watched her meet up with another Olive Ridley on a skateboard. After tying his board back on and adjusting his shell, Snap headed home.

The first half-mile wasn't so bad, but once Birmingham Street got steeper, the box shell turtle dropped to his hands and took it easy the rest of the way. *Dude, this upright walking sure isn't easy,* he thought as he noticed the pain in his shins.

At home, Snap found his dad at work in the office, so he quietly passed by, trying not to bother him. He made himself a bowl of granola and fruit for dinner and took it to his bedroom. Snap powered up his laptop so he could start on his homework. He knew most of the surf terms on the paper, but he went on to his favorite surfing website to get the few he wasn't quite as sure about. He defined the different surf breaks: beach, point, and reef, and he ended with the section on the different kinds of air tricks you can perform on a board. "Piece of cake!" Once Snap was finished, he flipped on his favorite TV station, the Discovery Channel, and fell asleep to the sound of a waterfall and African Forest Elephants exploring the depths of the Tropical Rainforest.

Chapter 3
Such a Tourist

Snap woke up extra early to the rumble of the Coaster passing through town. The train's whistle blew as Snap stared at the ceiling in his dark room. The sun hadn't even come up, and the stars painted on his ceiling were still glowing in the dark. He crawled out of bed and walked outside to sit on his balcony overlooking Cardiff Beach. *Now this is the life,* Snap thought to himself as he rested his shell on one of the newly cleaned lawn chairs.

The summer breeze was fresh but chilly that early in the day, which was nothing like Galveston. He had always imagined California being much warmer than this. Past all the rooftops and palms, Snap focused on the reflection of the moon softly lighting up one area of the ocean. At that moment, Snap didn't have a care in the world. No balancing games or walking on two feet, no biker turtles, and no drama in sight.

Snap spotted a bale of turtles catching rides at the light of dawn. He knew that was the best time to surf the morning glass. He noticed one turtle was farther out than all the others. The picture was ultimate perfection. It could have been captured on a postcard or the cover of a movie. One single surfer crouched down, getting barreled in what looked like a five or six foot wave. Snap had a good feeling that turtle had to be Timmy. He imagined himself replacing the turtle in the photo worthy image. He'd give anything to ride like that.

Snap's determination encouraged him to take his flippers out of his shell and strap them on. He figured it wouldn't hurt to keep practicing his walk. Snap walked up to the edge of the balcony and leaned against the rail, continuing to take in the panoramic view.

"You're up early, son. Don't lean too far over the edge or you may fall!" Mr. Shell came outside with a bowl of fruit and granola balanced on the top of his shell.

Snap instantly dropped to all fours when he heard his dad's voice. "You scared me, Pops. I'm just checking out the view." Snap forced a smile as he looked at Mr. Shell standing on his hands and feet.

Mr. Shell eyed Snap's flippers. "What do you have your flippers on for?"

Snap didn't say a word, but Mr. Shell kept on. "It *is* a spectacular view. Want to eat breakfast out here?"

Snap wanted to get an early start out and explore a little more of Cardiff. He was actually hoping to catch up with Tula before class and get a tour of the beach.

"I'll just grab a banana, Pops. I've gotta practice before class."

"Oh, okay." Mr. Shell looked disappointed. "Need any help tying your board to your shell?"

"Oh, well, I can just carry it." Snap bit his lip in anticipation of what his dad might say next.

"Carry it?" his father asked. "How is that even possible?" Mr. Shell looked at his son with a crinkled brow, shaking his head, and sat down at the table to fix himself a bowl of cereal. Snap

Such a Tourist

slowly and with hesitation, propped himself back up onto his feet, tightening every muscle in his legs to balance and not fall in front of his dad. "See."

Mr. Shell was busy pouring granola in a bowl and didn't see his son standing up on his hind legs, at least not right away. When he finally looked up, he almost knocked the bowl off the table. "Oh my! What in the great puka are you doing?"

"I'm standing! I learned it for surfing, Pops. All the turtles here walk like this."

Mr. Shell held a face that looked like he had seen a ghost. "But they're sea turtles son. They're meant to walk that way. We're box shells."

"That's why I'm wearing my flippers. They help me balance."

Mr. Shell had nothing to say to that comment, but Snap noticed the look of disgust on his dad's face.

"Pops, it's not that big of a deal. I bet you could even do it," Snap said with a slight wobble and grabbed the railing.

"No, no, son. I've been walking this way my whole life. I have no desire to walk like a sea turtle."

"But isn't change good, Pops? It's not like I'm trying to *be* a sea turtle, I'm just learning some of the culture out here, that's all."

"There is no need for me to change now, but if you think you must walk that way, then…" Mr. Shell didn't finish his thought. The air on the balcony went still and the waves crashed in the distance. "I guess I'll go get you your banana, son." Mr. Shell got up and left the balcony, not saying another word or finishing his own breakfast.

Snap could tell his dad was having a hard time with the adjustment, but he didn't know what else he could do or say to get him to understand. Obviously his dad had no idea how hard it was to be different these days. He slowly walked inside to get his shell packed and ready for the day.

When Snap walked downstairs, Mr. Shell handed him a banana and a couple of dollars for lunch.

"Thanks, Pops." Snap hugged his dad good-bye, grabbed his board, and headed out the door.

"Don't forget to put sunscreen on the top of your head," his dad said softly.

"It's in my shell, Pops." Snap shut the door and walked slowly down the driveway, wondering if he had done something wrong. Didn't Mr. Shell know that Snap wasn't going to be just like him? Snap liked action, sports, fun, everything that his dad avoided, or so it seemed. Snap was just about to turn and pass the mailbox when suddenly…

"Boo!" A crabby French voice yelled from the other side of the mailbox.

Such a Tourist

"Ahhh!" Snap yelled. If it were possible for a turtle to jump out of his shell, he would have.

"Sorry *monsieur*. No need to be startled. Star here suggested we come by and bring you a fresh cup of morning coffee, straight from our favorite café shop, Starlucks Coffee."

"Gosh, Herbert, you really didn't have to," Snap said, and looked down at the starfish. Snap highly doubted Star made any type of suggestions whatsoever, being that he never spoke.

Before Snap could finish, Star jumped off Herbert's back and handed Snap his coffee.

Snap hesitated as he took the cup. He sniffed the opening and was instantly taken back to the familiar stale aroma of his fourth grade teacher's dog breath at Memorial Elementary. Mrs. Buff was an old terrier with a big coffee addiction. "Is there really coffee in here, or is it more like one of those frapa-something-chinos?"

Star nodded his head yes.

"Yes, it's coffee, or yes, it's a frapa-something-chino?" Snap asked.

"Allow me to translate," Herbert said. He studied Star closely with his bifocals and turned to Snap to say, "That means coffee."

"Dude, I'm only ten. I can function just fine without coffee. But thank you though." Snap placed the cup back on the ground next to Star. That move sent the starfish into hysterics, and he started bouncing from bush to tree to mailbox, spilling coffee all over himself and the street. Finally, the crazed starfish landed on one of his five hands on a rough rock used as a decoration in the front yard. Snap could never tell which of Star's appendages were used as a hand, foot, or head the way he bounced around so much.

"Come now, Star. No need to act like a crazy gull. Get up and show our friend some manners," Herbert said. Star picked himself off the rock and returned to Herbert's shell, leaving one of his arms or maybe it was a leg behind on the ground.

Snap's eyes bulged at the sight of the body part. *Dude!* The crab and starfish walked away quickly as if they had no idea they were leaving a body part on the ground. Snap's refusal to drink coffee must have really offended the little crustaceans. "Hey! You left your arm!" Snap yelled, looking back down at the arm, wiggling around like a lizard tail. He stood there trying to decide whether or not to return Star's arm to him.

"Hmm. If my arm was lying on the ground, would I expect someone to hold onto it?" Snap said out loud. "Probably not." The turtle quickly picked up the body part with his thumb and index finger as it wiggled profusely. Nearly dropping it, he attempted to throw it in his mailbox for safe-keeping, but before the appendage made it, a seagull swooped down from out of nowhere and snatched it in midair.

"Hey! That was a starfish arm...I mean leg...I mean part!" Snap yelled up to the seagull. "Bring that back!"

The seagull let Snap know what he thought about that by leaving a splattered surprise on the Shell's driveway.

"Yuck! Totally uncool dude!" Snap shook his head and slowly walked down the street. There was little he could do about Star's appendage now. He imagined the poor little starfish holding onto Herbert's shell, one limb missing. *What a way to start his morning*, he thought. First his dad and now this. Snap was ready to relieve his stress down at the beach and hopefully, find Tula. He pulled out the map Trekker had given him and walked in the direction of Pipes surf break, carefully taking in his surroundings. He couldn't help but notice on all of his walks that the town was obsessed with surfing. There were turtles with surfboards and skateboards

Such a Tourist

everywhere. Even the "turtle crossing" signs had turtles with boards.

"Hey, stranger!" Snap's thoughts were interrupted.

"Tula, I was looking for you!" Snap shouted.

"You were?" she smiled.

"Well, I mean, I was hoping to meet up and well, you know, maybe you show me around, but it's not like I was *looking*, looking for you."

"Alright, Boxy, let me break it down for you." Tula took Snap farther up the hill so they could get a good view of the coastline.

"Do you have to call me Boxy?" Snap said and huffed up the hill.

"Sorry. I'm just kidding. But I need you to pay attention." The look in Tula's eyes told Snap that his tour was about to become a lesson. "See that break over there," Tula pointed down to the left where the good waves were starting to form just in front of the bridge. "That's Cardiff Reef. Most Olive Ridley bales surf over there, but on a good swell, the Leatherbacks usually kick us out."

"So, no one really gets along with the Leatherbacks?"

"You mean, sea scum? That's right. Stay clear of them, they're nothing but trouble. And Cardiff Reef is still their territory."

"Is there anything else I should know?"

"Hmm." She tapped her flipper on her chin. "Oh, don't talk too loud when you're around a gull. You ever heard the expression, *a little birdie told me*?

"Yeah."

"Well, on the beach, the gossip queens and kings are gulls! And one in particular," she continued, "Gill!"

"Seagulls? Dude." Snap thought about the gulls down in Texas and how they seemed harmless.

"Yep. Air scum is what I like to call them."

"Wow, y'all really don't like each other around here. I mean every gull and every Leatherback can't be bad. Isn't that like, well, discrimination?"

"Ha, ha. Y'all. Such a Texan." Tula giggled imitating Snap's Texas slang. "But, seriously, Snap. Do you not remember what happened yesterday? Trust me on this one. You'll learn quickly. No one here is as they seem. You've gotta watch out for yourself man." Tula nodded her little head while catching sight of an empty seaweed soda can on the ground, which she quickly grabbed and kept going.

Snap just nodded, not sure how to take what she said.

"Now," Tula continued. "Straight in front of us, you know, where the surf school is, that surf break is called, Pipes. And the famous Swamis break is just down there in Encinitas." Tula pointed her flipper to the right, and Snap noticed large groups out in the ocean, surfing at the point.

The two turtles kept walking and talking, Snap lowering his voice every time they passed a seagull. He felt like he was becoming paranoid with all of Tula's rules.

"So you're walking pretty good on those flippers, huh?" Tula took a moment to compliment Snap's ability to keep up with her this time but didn't break for long and kept on with the lesson. "Now Cardiff is a surf town, as I'm sure you can tell by now. The locals hang here. We practice riding around Pipes and Swamis, but all the big waves go off at Huntington and Trestles. The surf there is so legit. They're both just north of here."

"Wait, can you show me on the map?" Snap unfolded his trusty map.

Such a Tourist

"Such a tourist." Tula laughed again. "I'll show you, but you have to promise not to pull that thing out when we're around the other turtles on the beach." She grabbed his map to point out the spots. "Where in the world did you find this old thing? It looks like some ancient souvenir or something."

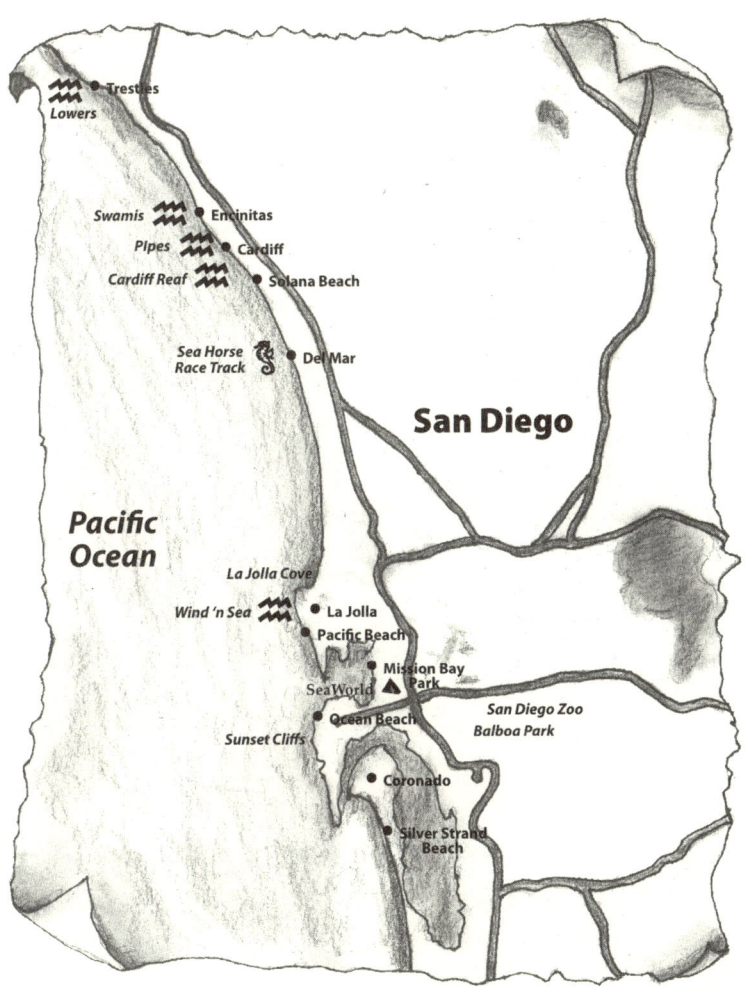

"I don't know. Trek gave it to me." Snap hovered over Tula while she pointed to the breaks out at Cardiff and Trestles. Tula handed back his map, and Snap studied the surf breaks.

"Hey!" Tula screamed.

Snap turned and jumped back just in time before getting plowed into by a family of turtles on a beach cruiser.

"Watch where you kids are going!" The turtle mom yelled from the passenger seat.

"Sorry." Snap waved his map in apology.

"Forget them. Just keep your peripherals on guard, man. You don't really see too many of those out here anyway. Mostly in La Jolla where the family activities are." She shrugged and threw away the litter she had collected on their walk into a trashcan at the corner.

"Too many of what? Beach cars?" Snap asked while looking for La Jolla on his map.

"No, silly. You, know, families? Parents? Kids?"

"What are you talking about?" Snap said, confused as he folded up his map.

"Hardly any of the turtles here have parents," Tula said.

"What? No one? You don't have a mom or dad?"

"Of course I've got a pair. They're just not here right now, but they'll be back soon. Or my mom at least. I mean we *are* sea turtles if you haven't noticed."

"Believe me, I can't help but notice." Snap stood there for a moment in contemplation and then remembered something, "So, it really is true? Sea turtles just lay their kids' eggs on the beach and leave them? Alone?"

"Yep. It's not like a tortoise, I suppose. It's all a part of our inner puka. We know what we are...what to do. Our parents lay their eggs and pray a crazy gull doesn't snatch us up when we hatch.

Such a Tourist

Urrr, those good for nothing gulls!" Tula started to get riled up. "I've probably lost a hundred brothers and sisters to the birds, if I counted."

"What, a hundred, that's impossible?" Snap gasped. His head was spinning from all the information Tula was sharing. Life in California was much different than the suburbs of Texas.

"Come on Snap, you can't be serious. Sea turtles can lay hundreds of eggs."

Snap must not have watched that episode about his native ancestors on the Discovery Channel. Of all the things his father *didn't* tell him.

"That's why I'm part of the Sea Turtle Society. We help out the baby eggs when they hatch and keep the beaches clean, of course. It's just the turtle thing to do, you know. Do you realize how many plastic bags get washed into our ocean? You should totally join."

"Do you help all of the baby turtles, even the Leatherbacks?"

"Yes, even the Leatherbacks," Tula laughed. "All eggs are innocent until proven guilty, that is until they reach adolescence and drive mopeds."

Snap wasn't sure how to ask his next question, but he felt, since Tula was so open about everything else, it wouldn't matter much. "So where are your parents anyway?"

"Well." Tula took a moment to dramatically sigh and shake her head. "My mom's in Hawaii right now, but she *should* be back any day. Most of the adult sea turtles travel the ocean. Some become actors out at Sea World or the Zoo or serve in the military, that sort of stuff." She thought about her response for a moment, then said, "You know dude? My father is a drill instructor or something like that in the Aquatic Marines. I haven't seen him since I was a baby, to be honest."

"So your dad's in the military and your mom is a...?"

"She's an underwater guide in Ohau." Tula could tell Snap wanted to know more, so she continued, "I've only been in Cali for a few years. I was born in Costa Rica. Lived there since I was seven. When my flippers were strong enough for the swim, my mom moved me and my older brother, Spike, to the West Coast. She knew the school programs here were pretty good and the elders were well respected. You see, the elders take care of us while our parents are working around the ocean. That's their job if they don't want to entertain or serve the country, I guess."

The turtles stopped in front of the train tracks at the bottom of the hill and waited for the Coaster to pass.

"Dude, so was that the last time you saw your mom?" Snap asked.

"Huh? Sorry, I can't hear you?" Tula yelled as the train let out a loud whistle.

"I said," he yelled, "your mom, was that the last time you saw your mom?"

"Yeahhhhhh. I don't know what's taking so long for her to come back." Tula kept yelling as the train passed by. "She promised that one day we could go with her to Hawaii."

Snap stared at Tula for a moment while the Coaster chugged by. As he studied her side profile, he noticed she was either wearing some sort of blush or her cheeks were turning pink.

When the train finally passed, the pair crossed the tracks.

Tula continued talking, but this time her voice was much softer. "She was supposed to come back for my eleventh birthday."

"How old are you?" Snap couldn't help but ask.

"Eleven." She looked down at her flippers.

"I'm sorry." Snap knew what it was like to miss a mom.

"It's been over three years since I've seen her," she said quietly and started to pick up the pace again.

Tula was a year older than Snap, and she hadn't seen her mom for almost the same amount of time as he hadn't seen his own mother. He couldn't help but wonder if her mom was okay. Why would she break a promise to her daughter? Thinking about it, naturally made him think of his own mother and how much he knew she would have enjoyed California.

The turtles from their class started to gather near the surf school. "Is it time for class yet?" Snap asked, hoping to get his mind off the topic of moms.

"Nah, but let's go say hi to some of the bale. Come on!" Tula perked back up. "You'll feel at home in no time, I promise." She ran out in front of Snap and then looking back she said, "Just leave the map in your shell dude!"

Snap Gets Dreadlocks

Tula and Snap strolled down to the beach, heading straight toward a group of turtles, who appeared to be Olive Ridleys. They all basically looked like Tula, pointed beaks, green shells and skin, and they were very petite compared to the other sea turtles. Every single one of them had a skateboard too.

Snap looked down near the surf shop and noticed a group of Hawksbill turtles gathered around, laughing and pointing at each other. Down the way, closer to the water, Lucas was standing in the middle of a bale of Leatherbacks, and he appeared to be telling stories, pointing and gesturing as he talked. Snap continued to notice that each group of turtles seemed to hang out with only their own kind.

The pair continued walking until they reached the bale of Olive Ridleys in deep conversation. Their speech seemed so foreign to Snap.

"Ah, brah, the surf was so flat at Lowers yesterday. I was totally bummed. It was all mushy and stuff, ya know?"

"Bummer... you should have been here yesterday. It was going off at Swamis. Epic, brah, epic."

"Ah, man. I bet you were stoked."

"Hey, you know, brahs, Timmy is going tow-in up north at the spot in a few weeks. We heard 'em say it, man."

"No way! Catching some double overhead! Think he'll let us go?"

Tula butted in, "Hey guys. You remember Snap, right?" She knew their talk would go on for days.

One turtle spinning a skateboard on its side managed to offer a kind of hello.

"Wud up?" He nodded his head, revealing an interesting looking spiked necklace. Snap thought they might be shark teeth.

"Awesome necklace, dude," Snap said.

"That's Spike, my brother," Tula said.

"Oh hey, it's nice to meet you." Snap held out his hand for a shake, and Spike bumped it with his flipper.

Tula pointed out the rest of the turtles. "This is Mossy, D. J. Slide, and Barney's over there."

Snap Gets Dreadlocks

Snap looked over at the turtle they called Barney, who sneezed then snorted.

Snap turned to Tula and asked if he was okay.

"Shhh. Barnacle has allergies," she said.

"Barnacle?" Snap looked back over at Barney and noticed all of the barnacles stuck to his shell. *Gross,* he thought. As he looked even closer, he noticed Mossy was covered in green slime, and the one they called D.J. Slide, well, he wore his shorts so low Snap wondered why he wore any at all. *Where did these turtles come from?* Snap thought.

"Ahh, check it out," Spike said. "Look at the little dude's necklace."

All the turtles stared at Snap's necklace and for a moment, he wasn't sure if they were mocking him or actually admiring his puka shells.

"Cool, necklace, brah. Wrinklebutt used to have one just like it," Spike said.

Snap's heart skipped a beat when he heard the name *Wrinklebutt,* and instantly remembered his strange dream.

"Who's, Wrinklebutt?" his best friend asked.

"Wrinkle what?"

"I don't know, you were the one who kept saying it."

Snap gulped. "Um, who did you say had this necklace?"

"Wrinklebutt, man! Just the sweetest surfer this side of the Pacific. Well until she left that is," Spike said, while the rest of the bale nodded in agreement, even Tula.

"I'd almost ask where ya been dude," Tula started, "but I know the answer to that one." She winked at Snap. "You're right Spike. I can't believe I didn't notice it before. It's just like hers." Tula walked up to Snap Shell and leaned in to get a closer look at his necklace. "It even has the symbol!" she said.

"What is that symbol called again, Spike?"

Snap didn't hear a word Tula was saying, and a chill came over his body. He started to fade in an out of the moment, seeing the image of his dream he had back in Texas as clear as if the moment just occurred. He remembered the ocean and the huge turtle, who he actually thought was a guy, not a girl. He remembered the necklace, the waves, his mother, the flashes, everything. Was it possible Snap somehow dreamt about a real turtle he never met, or was it a crazy case of *déjà vu*?

"Snap. You okay? You look a little pastel." Tula started fanning him.

"Um, yeah, just didn't know Wrinklebutt was a girl, that's all."

"Does that surprise you? Chicks can surf just as good as dudes!" Tula snapped a finger in front of Snap's face and backed away.

"Not if I have anything to do with it," a deep voice from behind said.

Tula quickly turned around to find Lucas eavesdropping on their conversation. He was accompanied by two pesky seagulls squawking with laughter as if the words that came out of Lucas' mouth were somehow funny.

Spike stepped in to defend his sister. "What, are you actually going to surf with us today? This is school, you know. Thought you were too good to be seen around Pipes."

"Let me see that necklace." Lucas walked up to Snap and glared. "It's a fake. You all can quit your day-dreaming. Besides this B.T. is the biggest poser in California right now. I can't wait to see him surf. Why else do you think I came to class today?" Lucas pushed past Snap with a laugh, nearly knocking him over.

"Can you believe him, Snap? He called you a poser!" Tula said.

Snap Gets Dreadlocks

Snap didn't seem to care about the insult, because all he could think about was how ironic it was that Spike said Wrinklebutt had a necklace just like his. Why would he have a dream about a turtle who he had never met, or even knew existed?

"So, where is Wrinklebutt?" Snap asked the bale, hoping to get more details.

"She just disappeared one day. Vanished, brah. No one knew why or where she went." Slide said, shrugging his shoulders.

"No note. Nothing. It's a mystery, man." Spike started eyeing Snap's necklace again.

"It's been almost three years since anyone has seen her, brah," Mossy said, waxing his board.

"Rumor has it she swam to Mexico to get married," Spike said with a laugh, nudging his sister.

"No she didn't." Tula pushed her brother away. "Something made her leave. At least, that's what I think."

Spike whispered to Snap, "Wrinklebutt was Tula's role model."

Snap wanted to bring up his dream but was afraid no one would believe him. He noticed Timmy come out of the surf shop and head toward their spot in the sand. Class was about to start.

Knowing Timmy's assistants would be trailing just behind him, Snap thought about Star and worried whether his arm stub was healing properly.

Timmy walked up to Snap and the Olive Ridley bale. "Dudes! And dudette." Timmy winked at Tula. "What's the topic of convo?"

"Oh, nothing." Tula and all the turtles got quiet and chose not to mention they were talking about Wrinklebutt.

"Well, it's time for some riding. It's another big swell today. Ready to get inside the curl, kids?"

Tula looked over to Snap. "That means there are going to be a lot of good waves."

"I know what a swell is!" Snap said defensively.

"What about a curl?"

"Of course I know what a curl is. This lizard, on my baseball team, Cooper, his tail used to do it all the time. Usually when he was up to something."

"What are you talking about?" Tula asked.

"It was a joke."

"Oh," she shrugged. "We're talking about waves, silly. It's the part of the wave you always want to be in. You'll see."

Snap knew Tula had no idea how much he actually knew about surfing, or rather, how much time he spent on Turtle Tube watching surf videos and how many magazines he read. He rolled his eyes at her and smiled, gathering his board along with the rest of the students.

Snap watched as Tula grabbed her board and ran straight past the Leatherbacks for the water, duck diving into the waves ahead. Within seconds, she had paddled out into the water on her belly. She turned to face him and the rest of the class as a wave approached over her right shoulder. With perfect precision, the wave pushed her forward and broke to the left as she hopped to her feet to catch it.

Tula rode the wave all the way in to the beach until she stopped right in front of Snap.

All Snap Shell could say was, "Dude!"

"Did you see it? Did you see it?" She hopped off her board and nearly knocked Snap over.

"What, you showing off? Yes, I did," Snap said.

"No, the curl!" Tula said while turning her head to give Lucas the stink eye.

"Nice demonstration, Tula." Timmy motioned for all the turtles to come together to start class, and Snap noticed Lucas leave the group and head down toward the bridge. Timmy looked around. "I feel like I'm forgetting something," he said. "Oh, has anyone seen my assistants?"

Snap froze and didn't know whether or not to admit he saw them this morning and that Star was probably at the hospital.

"They did come by my house this morning," Snap whispered to Tula.

"For what?"

"Coffee?" Snap shrugged his shoulders.

"I'm not surprised." Tula shook her head. "Those two are totally crazy!"

"I still don't know how they found out where I lived." Snap paused for a moment, trying to decide how to explain what happened next. "I think Star got offended when I told him I didn't drink coffee, because..."

"*Bonjour!*" The French crab interrupted. Herbert crept up to Timmy with Star happily stuck to his back, all arms, legs, and head perfectly intact.

Snap couldn't believe his eyes. *How could that be?* He was certain Star's arm was sitting in the belly of a gull.

"But...but..." Snap wasn't sure how to ask such a personal question to someone who was already highly emotional. When Star saw him, he peeled his face away from Herbert's back, nodded a hello as casual as if nothing ever happened, then he returned to sucking on the hermit crab's shell.

Timmy picked up his surfboard and said, "You're late, Herbert. We were about to leave you two behind."

"Sorry, *monsieur*," Herbert bowed, and the starfish fell from his back. "I was printing out more business cards in case anyone needed more to hand out to friends and family. I charge by the hour in case anyone is interested in my services." Herbert moved alongside Timmy.

"No soliciting to the students, Herb." Timmy said. "Anyway, we are going to start class at Cardiff Reef and work our way back," Timmy announced. The turtles picked up their boards and followed. Once they got to the bridge, Timmy stopped and faced the ocean, while Herbert walked around asking for everyone's homework. All of the turtles copied Timmy's moves. No one spoke a word, made a sound, or even looked around.

The turtles stared straight ahead at the waves breaking on the shore. As Snap meditated on the sound of the ocean, he thought about the years he and his mom sat on the beach together in perfect silence, watching the waves come in. In this moment, he was able to practice the act of serenity she taught him by being still. He watched and observed how the waves seemed to repeat the same patterns, always breaking in the same place.

Timmy started to speak in a calm voice. "Keep your eye on the farthest spot. Three, two, here she comes." A wave bigger than all the others formed a wall, and next an inner barrel-like tube and a big turtle entered from the back, crouched down and surfed his way through. It was absolutely euphoric, and everything Snap had imagined, until he recognized the turtle who just rode the perfect wave. *Lucas!* No one made any comments. No one took their eyes off him or the surf as they watched in amazement. Snap realized how good Lucas really was and knew why he acted so tough with his bad leather vest and *Tortuga* Board.

"Yuck!" Tula moaned.

Snap wasn't as concerned with the Leatherback as he was with how Timmy knew that perfect wave was going to happen. Timmy stood up and all the turtles followed. Lucas rode in to the shore with an arrogant look on his face and jogged up to meet the rest of the class.

"Get back in line," Timmy said under his breath as Lucas passed him by.

Timmy turned around to face his pupils, and Snap stumbled to stand up and balance himself.

"Can anyone tell me which way the wave broke?" Timmy asked.

Slide raised his flipper. "Left."

"Correct. Would any of you do anything different out there?"

"Well, Lucas' knees were a little stiff." Spike called out.

"Agreed, dude. Agreed." Timmy nodded.

Lucas grunted in Spike's direction. "I'd like to see you try."

"And his vest was a little tight." Tula added, intentionally interrupting Lucas' remark to her brother. "Someone's been eating a few too many jellyfish!"

Lucas threw a string of seaweed, straight at Tula's back shell.

"Gross!" She threw it right back at him, accidently hitting a seagull flying low to the ground.

"Squawk!"

"Right on, right on," Timmy laughed. "Now, does anyone know why the waves are breaking all the way out there?"

Snap was pretty sure he had this one. "There's a reef out there?"

"Way to go, Boxy." Tula nudged Snap's shell.

Snap gave Tula a look when she called him by the nickname she made up, *again*.

"I know, I know. I'll lay off." She whispered back to him.

Timmy complimented Snap's answer. "Exactly. There's a reef out there," Timmy said and continued, "you'll see the waves break in the same place. A surfer must know the wave, know where it will break and when it will break. The reef also determines the shape of the wave." Timmy addressed the entire class and said, " So Snap was correct. That was a reef break."

Timmy picked up his board and started walking backward toward Pipes surf break. He continued talking as they walked back to the surf school.

"Snap, what kind of surf break is Pipes?" Timmy kept on with the pop quiz.

"Um, a beach break," he yelled so everyone could hear.

"Good deal. And that's where we will be learning today." Once Timmy found the perfect spot, he gave a few more minutes of

Snap Gets Dreadlocks

instruction and walked toward the water. Everyone did the same, including Herbert and Star. Trekker came out of his shop with a short board and handed it to Timmy, trading his old one with the new one. Trekker made custom boards and apparently just finished a new board, ready to be tested.

"Thanks, Trek. Just in time!" Timmy inspected the board and gave Trekker a nod.

"No problem, Tim. Have a nice ride, kids!" *Phfff.* Trekker waved and walked back to his shop, carrying Timmy's old board on top of his helmet.

Still amazed by the scientific device the lizard wore on his head, Snap watched him walk away, returning to his shop.

"Eyes on me." Timmy raised his flipper.

Snap's head darted back in Timmy's direction.

"Remember what we practiced yesterday. When the wave comes, turn to face the shore, stay back to avoid pearling, and hop up when you feel the force under your board pushing you up. Keep your boards turned parallel with the wave when you ride. Oh, and if you need wax, ask the crab."

"Um, Timmy, you know I didn't get to practice hopping up yesterday?" Snap said while raising his hand.

"You'll be fine little buddy." Timmy motioned for everyone to keep coming forward while he worked to wax his new board.

"Don't forget to leash up," Tula reminded Snap. "You don't want to lose your board when you hit the water."

Right, Snap thought. He tied the strap from his board to his ankle and double-checked it to make sure it was secure. As soon as Snap's blue flippers hit the water he laid face down on his board and paddled out, Tula to his left, Spike to his right. He couldn't believe he was actually in the ocean *and* on a surfboard. Timmy paddled out a few feet in front of the bale with

Herbert leading the way at the front of his board like a captain of his ship.

When they reached their destination in the water, Snap Shell eyed a good wave beginning to form, so he turned his board to prepare to surf his first wave. This was it. The moment he had been waiting his whole life for was suddenly here.

"It's all you, Snap," Timmy said, pointing at the box shell.

He squinted and looked back at the wave, a slow forming two-foot wave, but to Snap it seemed enormous. "Now, Timmy? Now?" Snap yelled back.

"Now!" Timmy yelled forward.

The wave took Snap's board. He panicked and the wave popped his board out from under his flippers and up in the air, leaving him face down in the white water. He came up for air, confused, startled and unsure which way was up and which way was down. He had a collection of seaweed hanging from his head.

"Sweet dreadlocks, B.T!" Lucas yelled as he coasted by Snap, riding his wave perfectly toward the shore. "Maybe you should stick to dry land, tortoise!" He yelled.

Snap Gets Dreadlocks

Snap shook off the seaweed and got right back on his board, determined to try again. He paddled back out to the bale of Olive Ridleys waiting on their boards, catching some sun.

"It's cool, brah. Everyone's gotta have their first wipe out." Timmy reassured him. "You just flipped out. Stay calm next time. No pressure man. We're surfing!"

Timmy was right. Snap just needed to find himself some zen.

"Here she comes, brah. Get ready."

Snap turned to see a nice wave forming. "Duuude!" Snap knew this one was going to be good, and he was excited to try again.

"Your wave, man!" Timmy called it for Snap. "To the right," Timmy yelled.

"Ok."

"He'll get this one, just watch," Timmy whispered to Tula who was sitting next to him observing her new friend.

Snap hopped up, right foot forward, his back shell to the face of the wave, keeping his knees nicely bent and staying in the curl as not to be too far in the white water. He was actually doing it.

"Hmm. He rides like me." Timmy smiled.

"Goofy foot?" Tula questioned.

"Yep."

Snap rode for so long, in order to keep going, he pumped the wave and changed positions a few times, to the left then back to the right. Trying to generate a little more speed, he began walking up and down on his long board.

"Is he walking the board?" Tula squinted, shielding the sun from her eyes.

"He's a natural, Tula. I saw it in his eyes yesterday," Timmy said. "Not to mention, the necklace. You know where that came from, right?"

"Huh?" Before Tula had a chance to continue, Timmy disappeared under water and popped up just in time to catch a big wave.

Tula caught the next one and rode it in to catch up with Snap who was now on the beach. "That was a gnarly ride! How did you know what you were doing?" Tula asked.

"I don't know," Snap said. "I just went with it. It was the sweetest feeling ever! I can't believe I got up."

"Got up? You like performed three or four different tricks on your first ride. You were so legit."

"I was?"

"Um, yeah!"

"Seriously. It was just one ride. I think I got lucky."

"No, I'm serious, Snap. You're like a natural or something. I've never seen a…a…" Tula fumbled to find the right words. "A new guy ride like that his first time in the water." Tula paused for a moment and eyed Snap's necklace. With a questioning look on her face she asked, "Are you sure you've never surfed before?"

"Tula. I just learned how to stand up. Do you think I would pose as a wannabe? Seriously, look at my feet. I have to wear flippers!"

"It's just weird. I mean, I don't want to sound rude, but you're a land turtle, yet it's like you know the water."

"Well, let's go back and see if it was just beginner's luck." Snap grabbed his board and started running toward the water with Tula following.

It definitely wasn't beginner's luck. Snap moved with the waves like he had been surfing for years. In his mind he actually had been surfing for years. He wanted it so bad. He had done his research, preparing for the day he would surf. He studied the ocean, the

Snap Gets Dreadlocks

weather and promised himself after his mom's death that he would never give up on his dream.

"Nice ride, goofy foot! Someone needs to enter the SWSHA conference." Timmy came up from behind the two turtles on their last ride in.

"He would totally be the first tortoise to ever enter a surf competition!" Tula jumped up.

"Well, not the first, but maybe the first to win." Timmy smiled.

"What is the SWS, um A...anyway?" Snap asked out loud. He then turned to Tula and asked in a whisper, "What's a goofy foot?"

"South West Surfing Honors Association!" Tula clapped her hands as she said each word then told Snap she would explain the *goofy foot* comment later.

"Surf Barrel 39! You got good grades, brah?" Timmy asked.

"Yeah. I mean I made all A's in 4th grade."

"You're in then. Gotta have at least a B plus average to compete."

"Do it!" Spike spoke up. "I would, but I made a C in math last year."

"What do I have to do?"

"Just follow me to the surf shop, and I'll get you the papers. We may need to do something about that board, though. It's a little long for what I'm about to teach you." Timmy patted Snap on the head and motioned for him to follow.

"I'll come too," Tula said. Snap followed Timmy and Tula, board in hand, and his head held high as he passed by the bale of Leatherbacks. Lucas didn't have anything to say to him after those last few rides either, which made him feel good.

Walking through the door to the surf shop, Snap read the sign on the door: TREK'S BOARDS AND MORE. Snap could see hundreds of surfboards all lined up, different colors, brands, shapes, and sizes.

"Come on in, brah. Take a look around," Timmy said.

The turtles headed up to the counter and found Trek's helmet lying on top. Trekker was missing in action. Snap leaned in to get a better look at the weird contraption and how it worked.

"Snap Snap!" Trekker jumped up from behind a long board he was shaping in the corner. What can I do for you?" *Phfff.* Trekker walked over to the counter to greet his customers.

"Why don't you have your helmet on?" Snap asked. He thought Trekker always wore his helmet.

"Well I don't need it in here." *Phfff.*

Now Snap was really confused. "But, why are you still making that sound?"

Trekker seemed lost. "What sound?" *Phfff.* Trekker obviously had no idea what Snap was talking about, or he was playing some kind of joke on him. Tula just giggled.

Timmy shook his head and changed the subject. "Snap Shell here needs some forms to enter the SWSHA Conference."

"Surf Barrel, huh? You must be pretty good if old Timmy thinks you can enter a surfing competition." Trekker pulled out a paper from underneath the cabinet.

"He's got the spirit. A couple of lessons with me, and he'll be ready." Timmy sounded pretty sure of himself *and* Snap's ability.

"He's awesome, Trek!" Tula confirmed.

"Here ya go, sonny. Just return the form back to me or Timmy." *Phfff.*

"Thanks!" Snap and Tula told Trekker and their instructor good-bye and headed out the door. Tula decided to walk all the way back to Snap's house, so she could look over the competition forms with him. Snap read the rules out loud, but one particular part took him by surprise.

"What? The first qualifying conference is only *one month away*?" He may have had a good first day in the water, but he knew that the turtles who competed in those things had been surfing for years. There was no way he would be ready in a few weeks.

"You'll be fine. Be more positive. You have a *whole month* to practice." Tula tried to reassure him.

He scanned down to the last few lines regarding the prizes. If he actually made it all the way to the Hawaiian Nationals, he could win a scholarship for college. Snap let out a snort as he struggled to walk up the hill and read.

"You okay?" Tula giggled.

Snap just nodded, not sure what he thought of it all. He didn't want to admit he was scared, but it just seemed too soon, too dangerous. The more and more he thought about why he shouldn't compete, the more he felt like his dad.

Once they reached Snap's house, Tula said good-bye and skipped back down the hill, leaving Snap to his own concerns. Snap thought about how easy it was for her to tell him to *just compete*, considering she wasn't the one who had to prove herself to a beach full of sea turtles. Snap had a lot to think about that night and the next morning before seeing Timmy and the other turtles again.

First Time for Everything

Saturday morning Snap woke up to chatter in the kitchen. He couldn't make out what was being said, but he was pretty sure he heard his name come up more than once. He rolled out of bed to see who his dad could have possibly invited to breakfast. Snap walked into the kitchen, still rubbing sleep from his eyes, shocked at who he found there with his father. "Tula? What are you doing here?" Snap hadn't even brushed his teeth yet.

"Good morning, sleepy head!" Tula said, just before taking a bite of a blueberry pancake. Tula's smile quickly changed to a questioning look when she noticed Snap was on all fours. "Why are you..."

"Shh." Snap cut her off with his finger over his lips and quickly took a seat next to her at the table. After the way his dad acted yesterday, Snap considered taking the *hands to feet* transition slowly. "What are you doing here, any..."

Mr. Shell cut him off. "Someone woke up on the wrong side of the shell this morning," he said while setting a plate in front of Snap. "Tula here has been telling me all about your performance in the waves yesterday."

"She did?" Snap cringed and gave Tula the stink eye when Mr. Shell turned to grab some maple syrup for his son's pancakes. Tula sure didn't have a problem making herself at home in Snap's kitchen. Even if he didn't want to admit it, he kinda liked her persistent style, but he felt more comfortable acting annoyed.

"Why didn't you tell me how your classes were going?" Mr. Shell asked.

"Um," Snap started while he nervously fumbled with his pancakes. "Just getting used to all the changes, Pops." Snap was hoping Tula hadn't said anything about the surf competition yet, but before he knew it...

"Yeah, he's even going to compete!"

"What?" Mr. Shell looked directly at his son.

"No I'm not."

"But you got the..."

Snap cut her off. "I'm not going to compete. The competition is too soon. Besides I'm just learning. It's just for fun, right Pops?"

Mr. Shell agreed, "Tula, Snap knows better than to get himself involved in silly competitions. School will be starting in a month, *and we both* agreed school is more important than surfing."

Tula didn't say a word. Snap avoided making eye contact with her.

Mr. Shell shook his head and got up again to start washing his dish. "So what are you kids up to today?" He changed the subject.

"Oh!" Tula jumped up from her chair. "That's why I came over! I wanted to see if Snap wants to swim down to Pacific Beach. Some of the bale are going to Belmont Park later today, and we're going to have a bonfire at Mission Bay tonight."

So, there *was* a reason for Tula suddenly dropping by for breakfast. Snap pulled out his map and laid it across the table.

First Time for Everything

"That all sounds like a lot of fun, but..." Mr. Shell started with a very concerned look on his face. "Isn't that a far swim for a box turtle to hold his breath? Maybe you should take the Coaster."

Snap wasn't quite sure how he would make that trip underwater either and waited for Tula's response.

"Not if Snap uses a Sea Trek Helmet! Well, at least until he learns to hold his breath." Tula grinned.

To Snap's surprise, his dad knew exactly what Tula was talking about. "Hmm. I mean you *are* right. A Sea Trek Helmet *would* work. And Snap has been using his flippers all summer."

"Timmy is meeting us there, too. He's our surf instructor. Timmy Turtle."

Great idea, Snap thought. Surely if his father knew an adult turtle would be there, he would feel more comfortable with Snap going. Tula seemed to have a way with parents for not being around them much.

"Timmy Turtle, huh? I don't see why not. As long as he doesn't try to get you to enter that competition!" Mr. Shell said with his hands on his hip shell.

What? Snap couldn't believe she got him to say yes. But how could anyone say no to a cute little Olive Ridley? Good thing Mr. Shell never had a girl, or he would have been whooped.

"I'm not entering, okay Pops?" Snap sat at the table eating his pancakes and smiled at Tula who was looking very confused. Her beak pointed down in disappointment. "Let me just pack my shell and we can leave," Snap said, his mouth stuffed with pancakes. Snap finished his last syrupy bite and walked back to his room. "Do I need my board?" He yelled from inside his bedroom.

"Nah! It's going to be flat out today!" Tula yelled back. Snap packed up his shell with all the necessary supplies for the day—his blue visor, sunscreen, flippers, protein bar, map and a few dollars from his allowance jar. After waxing his shell and washing his face in the bathroom, he noticed Tula in his room through the bathroom mirror, messing with his stuff.

"Who's this in this picture with you?" Tula was now making herself at home in Snap's bedroom and studying a picture of Snap on his dresser.

"Which one, nosey?" Snap walked over to inspect the frame she picked up. "Oh, Iggy? That's my best friend from back home."

"And in the tree?"

"Ha. That's his little sister, Molly. We took that picture before our district tournament game."

"I didn't know you played baseball!"

"Yep. Catcher!"

"Cute bracelets."

"Okay, Okay. They're armbands," Snap said, defending himself. "And they aren't *cute*. They catch sweat. Are you ready to go yet?"

"Yeah, I was just waiting on you to finish waxing your shell," she giggled.

"I'm finished. And why were you eavesdropping on me?"

"Why are you walking on your hands again?"

"Duuude! Don't say that so loud. I'll tell you outside. Let's just get out of here."

"After you." Tula held one flipper out toward the open door.

Once they were down the street, Snap stopped to put on his flippers and stood up on his back feet.

"Seriously? Do you not want your dad to see you vertical or something?" Tula quickly asked.

"He didn't exactly take my new balancing trick the way I'd hoped. But I'm not surprised."

"And the competition? Did you decide to give up that easily, or were you faking that, too?"

"No, that was real. What business do I have competing against guys like Lucas?"

"Um, dude, besides the fact you're good and will be great after a month of school and lessons?"

"Forget it Tula. You saw how my dad reacted to the mention of the word *surfing*. It's a joke to him. Plus, I need to be careful with all the changes and everything. He needs time to adjust."

"Adjust? Well, I bet the two of us could change his mind. He was really cool with me."

Snap stopped mid-stride and shook his head. "He's not cool, Tula. He's sensitive. His feelings get hurt when he thinks I don't want to be like him."

"But he's your dad. He's going to accept you for who you are, right?" Tula said.

"Tula," Snap paused, "you wouldn't understand."

"Why? Cause I don't have any parents around? It's not like I don't *know* my mom!"

"That's not what I meant. I promise."

"Then try me. What about your dad do you think I won't understand? I'm pretty sure my parents are divorced too. I mean they've been separated for as long as I can remember."

"No. I didn't mean it like that. I'm sorry. And they aren't divorced." Snap got quiet, not sure if he wanted to go any further into this conversation, but he knew he couldn't shut her out. She was just trying to help. "Okay." He paused and looked around, checking for gulls. "Well, after my mom died..."

"What?" Tula gasped. "I'm so sorry! I had no idea. Why didn't you tell me?" She stopped in the middle of the street.

"I am right now." Snap came to his own defense.

"Okay, right now you are. But I totally told you about my mom days ago. Why are you just now waiting to tell me about yours? Boys...you're all the same. Keeping everything in and always bringing things up at the wrong time."

"Tula. It was only yesterday, and stop getting so emotional. Do you want me to tell you or are you just going to yell at me?"

"You're right. Sorry." She took a second to relax her mind. "Ok. I'm listening."

The couple started walking again down to the beach, slowly this time.

"After it happened," Snap started.

"Wait!" Tula interrupted him again. "*When* did it happen?"

"Almost two years ago." Snap huffed when she cut him off for the second time.

"Sorry, sorry, keep going."

"I was eight. She was in a car accident." Snap paused and looked down at his blue flippers, remembering the past. His mother meant so much to him, so much more because she believed in him, his passions, his dreams, so much.

Snap watched Tula's eyes grow wide with curiosity and he continued. "The hardest part was seeing how sad it made Pops. We went to counseling, and everything started to get better, but I still worry that certain things I say or do will make him feel bad, like when I try to do things that are so different than him. I was so close to my mom, sometimes closer than I was to him. We just had so much more in common. I *know* that makes him sad. I just hate disappointing him."

Tula put her hand on Snap's shell. "Then it's time to rebuild your relationship with your dad. Let him really get to know you. Don't you think it makes him sad not to know you, even if you are different than him?"

First Time for Everything

Snap paused for a moment before responding, realizing she might be right. But for reasons he wasn't sure of, he couldn't bring himself to truly express his differences to his father. "I didn't think of it like that. He's just so busy with his research all the time, but maybe you're right."

"Of course I'm right," Tula said, bumping her shell against his.

"It's just not that easy. That's all."

"Well, at least you have a parent who is around and cares. I would give anything for my mom and dad to come back."

That comment made Snap feel guilty for shutting his dad out.

"You should at least try talking to him about the surf competition. Maybe if he actually *sees* you surf, he might change his mind."

"Let's just not talk about the competition for a little while, okay?" Snap asked.

The two turtles were silent the rest of the way to the surf shop.

When they arrived, Trekker was outside the shop spraying off rental boards and helmets. "Look who it is!" *Phfff.* "I knew you two would make a perfect pair."

"What?" Tula backed up. "Him?" She started laughing to the point it made Snap a bit uncomfortable.

"Come on Trek." Snap's cheeks started to blush. "She's just…"

"A friend?" Trekker asked. *Phfff.* "Uh, huh. Well, what can I do for you two individuals, then?" *Phfff.*

"We're going to Mission Beach, and Snap needs some gear," Tula said with a funny grin on her face.

What in the world is she thinking? Snap thought.

"Of course. Of course," Trekker said, his glass helmet filling with condensation. "It'll be twelve dollars for the day." *Phfff.*

"What? Twelve dollars? I only have five bucks for the entire day, and that includes money for lunch," Snap said.

Trekker looked him over and scratched the top of his helmet, which Snap thought was quite odd. "Okay. I'll take that then." *Phfff.*

"Dude, I said it's for lunch," Snap huffed. "And I thought you said the Turtle Board funds the stuff…"

Trekker cut him off. *Phfff.* "No, no, no. I said group activities. Yes, that's what I said, uh huh." *Phfff.*

"Come on Trek, can't you just give him a day for free? Sort of a welcome to town gift? He's new," Tula pleaded.

"Fine. You owe me though. The windows around the shop need a good washing to scrub the salt off of them." *Phfff.*

"Awesome. He'll wash next week," Tula promised for him.

"I will?"

Tula grabbed Snap by the hand to lead him inside to find the right helmet. Trekker followed behind the pair.

"Okay, kids, slow down. I'll find the perfect fit for old One Snap." *Phfff.* "Here you go sonny," Trekker said, handing Snap a medium sized helmet. *Phfff.* It was connected to a small backpack by a breathing tube. The three reptiles walked down to the shore so Trekker could give Snap a few pointers on how to use it properly. "Alright sonny," Trekker said as he adjusted the helmet on Snap's head. "Perfect." *Phfff.* "In the water you go!" He gave Snap an encouraging push.

Snap walked into the ocean until the water hit him at mid shell. Trekker followed closely behind the box shell turtle with Tula alongside him.

First Time for Everything

"This thing is heavy," Snap said from inside his helmet. He worried for a moment about the condensation problem Trekker was always having. He even tried to mimic the act of clearing the helmet. *Phfff.* He laughed to himself.

"No complaining. You won't feel a thing when you go under," Trekker told him. *Phfff.*

Tula smiled and gave Snap a wink.

Trekker handed Snap his pack. "Now you only have to worry about keeping upright and enjoy the view." *Phfff.*

"Upright? But can't I swim?" In his confusion, Snap readjusted the helmet and looked past Trekker at the vast ocean before him. *Amazing,* he thought.

"We can get you some scuba equipment next time my windows are dirty. For now, it's baby steps my friend. Baby steps. Now off you go." *Phfff.*

Tula patted Snap's shoulder and said, "You'll be ready in no time. Just trust me."

"Alright. You kids have fun." Trekker headed back to his shop.

"Okay, Boxy. You're about to get a close-up view of a whole new world under here."

Snap realized Tula was talking. Between the sound of the rushing water and the waves crashing on the shore, he started to hear her less and less as they walked out a bit further from the coastline. "Huh? You're going to have to talk a little louder." Snap knocked on his helmet. "I can't hear anything you're saying dude!"

"I said, are you ready?" she yelled.

"Stay steady?" Snap asked.

Tula leaned in closer to the glass bubble. *"Are you ready?"*

Snap reached down under the water and tightened his flippers. He was ready. "Let's do it!"

"That's the spirit. Now just follow me."

Turtle Town: The Inner Puka

"What are we going to see?" Snap asked.

"No, I said *follow me*!"

They started moving further away from the shore, a few steps at a time with Snap following Tula's every move.

"And just so you know, turtles have the right of way to the fish, but sharks, eels, stingrays, and whales are a different story. You've gotta stop and let them pass in front of you."

"Sharks feel rays in front of whale stores?" Snap was confused. He could hardly hear what she was saying.

Tula laughed and repeated herself.

"Sharks?" Snap gulped.

"Dude, just don't look at them in the eyes and you'll be fine. Don't worry! Oh, do you mind if we say hi to my friend, Suzzy? She's a seahorse."

Still unsure of what she was saying, Snap repeated what he thought she said again. "Your friend sued a seahorse? Why?"

"No! We're going to say hi to my friend Suzzy. *She's* a seahorse!"

"Oh! Well, I've never met a seahorse before." Snap smiled.

"Great. She's been racing in Del Mar all summer. She'll be happy we came by. That'll be our first stop."

Tula looked around and moved behind Snap to inspect his gear one last time and motioned for him to follow. "Try to stay close to me, but don't crowd my bubble."

"Your bubble? I'm the one in the helmet, not you."

"I mean my space, silly. I need room to guide you."

"Okay, okay, bossy! I'll be fine. You don't have to yell at me!" Snap shook his helmet and smiled, trying to calm his nerves as much as he tried to reassure her he was okay.

Tula went under and Snap followed. He naturally held his breath and closed his eyes.

First Time for Everything

"Hey!" Tula yelled, tapping on Snap's helmet. "You don't have to hold your breath, dude!"

"Snap realized his face wasn't wet and opened his eyes to see Tula right in front of him. He breathed out and looked around surrounded by an underwater world like nothing he had ever seen. Life moved as quickly and as gracefully as it did on the shore. Creatures of every kind were swimming, conversing and living all around him.

"Wow!" He lifted one flipper and began to walk on the sandy bottom. Tula swam next to Snap as he walked. "This is awesome!" he yelled, but Tula couldn't hear him through his helmet.

Tula grabbed Snap's hand and pulled him along. Schools of metallic fish swam around them. Starfish cart-wheeled across schools of pufferfish. Stingrays kept close to the bottom, avoiding Snap's flippers. Snap suddenly stopped and pointed out ahead at a few sharks slowly passing by. Tula smiled, knowing that Snap stopped to give them the right of way. The pair moved together, slowly, one step at a time along the ocean bottom, until they reached Del Mar.

The Del Mar Race Track was full of seahorses of every shape and color. Tula seemed to know exactly where to find Suzzy, so she led Snap directly to her stable. When the seahorse saw Tula, her tail uncurled with excitement. Tula and Suzzy hugged and Snap watched Tula as she explained to her friend who he was and what he was wearing. The seahorse nodded her head at Tula and gave Snap a wink. The pair stayed for a moment and chatted until Suzzy reminded them it was almost time for her to warm up for her race. Tula wished her good luck, and then she and Snap continued on their journey.

Turtle Town: The Inner Puka

Snap fell in love with the ocean in a whole new way. He thought being on top of the water was cool, but underneath it was even better.

Once the turtles finally got to Pacific Beach, Snap followed Tula to the shore until he could see the sky above him. He stood up out of the water realizing that his arms and legs had gone limp.

"How you holding up, Boxy?" Tula asked. "Do you need to sit down or something? I'm impressed. You really kept up."

"Ah, thanks. It wasn't so bad," Snap said, breathing heavily, trying to sound convincing.

"Whatever you say, tough guy. You can't fool me."

The turtles started walking toward the boardwalk as Timmy pulled up in his yellow and black convertible.

"Wow! Look! It's Timmy and Spike! Why didn't we just catch a ride with them?" Snap asked.

Tula laughed. "Admit it, you're beat!"

"Hey, what do ya know? It's my favorite students," Timmy yelled over the loud engine. "Well, besides Spike." Timmy nudged Spike,

First Time for Everything

hopped out of his ride, and helped Snap out of his gear. "We can just throw all this stuff in the back."

"Dude. You wore a Sea Trek helmet?" Spike walked around to say hi.

"Yep. All the way from Trek's shop."

"Way to go, brah. I respect that," Spike said as he tapped hands with Snap. "So did it fog up on you?"

"Nope."

"Totally weird," Spike said. "I guess Trek's just got some really hot breath." He shrugged and continued, "So, are you totally stoked for the bonfire tonight?"

Tula cut in, "I am! That is *if* Timmy tells ghosts stories again like last time."

"You got it, girl! But first, Snap and I have some business to take care of up in La Jolla," Timmy said.

"We do?"

"You all run along. We'll see you at the bonfire."

Business? Snap thought. Me?

"But, but..." Snap was really looking forward to riding the roller coaster at Belmont Park.

"Laters!" Spike waved and headed to the beach with his sister.

"Don't let Squirt tip you!" Tula yelled back to Snap.

"Who's Squirt? Tip what?"

"He's just a seal that likes to tip surfers off their boards for a laugh," Timmy explained.

"We're going surfing?" Snap wondered if Tula knew the whole time that Timmy was taking him surfing. *What a little sneak*, he thought.

"Totally. Just you and me little buddy. Time for your first *private* lesson."

"Seriously? Sweet!" Snap ran behind and jumped into the passenger seat of Timmy's ride. He looked around, inspecting the inside. It was a 1967 Camaro SS 350 with black leather interior and flame designs on the floor board. "This is such a sweet..." he started but gasped when he looked inside the cup holder. "Dude!" A starfish arm was floating inside a miniature Starlucks coffee cup.

"What's the matter, brah?" Timmy looked inside the cup. "Dang regenerating starfish. Always leaving his arms in my ride." Timmy grabbed the limb, inspected it, and tossed it outside.

"Regeneration? So it grows back?"

"Yeah, well all that caffeine he drinks makes those things grow back at triple speed. He leaves them all over the place."

Snap looked back at the limb on the ground, and before he knew it, a small pack of seagulls were fighting for it in the sand. "Another one goes to the gulls. That looked like Gill."

"They all look like Gill to me," Snap said.

Timmy revved the engine, put it in first gear, and the pair took off down the shoreline, jamming *Bird Marley* all the way to La Jolla. Snap enjoyed the breeze and counted the amount of lady turtles that waved and shouted as Timmy drove by them.

"You know a lot of animals, here, huh?" Snap yelled over the sound of changing gears and music playing loudly on the stereo.

"Huh? You like *Bird*?" Timmy looked over to Snap and handed him the disc case.

"Um. Totally dude. He was my mom's favorite." Snap gladly took the disc.

"Your dad's too. Back in the day." Timmy added.

"What? You know my dad?" Snap perked up.

"We've met a time or two."

"How? When?" Snap asked.

First Time for Everything

The combination of music and wind was so loud that it was hard for Timmy to hear him.

"When did you meet my dad?" Snap asked, again getting no response. Before he knew it, they were pulling up to Seal Rock.

"Check 'em out! The seals are out sunbathing today," Timmy said, slowing down to get a better look.

Snap looked over to a sand patch full of huge rocks and sunbathing seals basking and yawning in the heat.

"Now that's one lazy animal, if you ask me," Timmy joked and picked up speed as he passed through La Jolla Village.

"Was Squirt over there?" Snap asked. Snap didn't want to get knocked off his board later.

"I guess we'll find out soon enough." Timmy winked.

"I thought Tula said the surf was flat today?" Snap questioned, remembering he didn't bring his board.

"Out in Cardiff, but Wind n' Sea will have a good point break for a few hours." Timmy took the scenic route to get to Wind n' Sea Beach. There wasn't a cloud in the sky, and the weather felt perfect for some wave riding.

They parked, and Timmy hopped out and unloaded the two boards from the backseat of his car. One for him and one for Snap. Snap was excited to learn he would be riding one of Timmy's top-notch *Tortuga* Boards.

"I'll let you borrow this one until you win a short board at your competition next month."

"Timmy! I can't compete this soon. I didn't realize the competition was only a month away." Snap's thoughts went back to his dad at the mention of competing.

"Don't doubt yourself, dude. You're going to rip it up out there little buddy." Timmy handed Snap his first Tri-Fin short board. It was yellow with black stripes, just like his car. "Follow me." Snap and Timmy walked down to the break. "So where'd you get that gnarly necklace brah?"

Snap's mind was racing with questions. He had so many things to consider. How did Timmy, of all turtles, know his father? How could that be possible? He didn't want to annoy the turtle who was taking time out of his busy life with too many annoying questions. "Oh, this." Snap lifted up his necklace. "My mom gave it to me three years ago." Snap started to get a little worried, "You're not going to make me take it off to surf are you?"

"Nah...I'm sure your mom wouldn't want you to take it off. I can tell she meant a lot to you. I'm sure you'll pass it down one day too," Timmy said.

Snap wondered if Timmy somehow knew his mother was gone.

They walked down a path of sandy rocks to get to the beach. Only a few turtles were out taking advantage of the swell.

"Why aren't there more surfers here?" Snap asked.

"That's the point. We need room. And this is *locals only*, my friend," Timmy said.

"But I'm not..."

"Shh. Doesn't matter brah. You're with me, so you're in."

Snap realized Timmy was right, and it was apparent everyone knew him. Not one animal failed to nod at Timmy each time they passed the green sea turtle.

Once they got past the rocks, Timmy told Snap to lay his board down and study the waves. "Just relax your mind, man. Nothing but you and the wave. Visualize yourself out there on the water."

"Snap took in the sound of the ocean, water rushing to his feet and a cool breeze carrying each surfer's spirit back to their own wave. The surfers at the point were good, each one totally flowing with the motion of the sea. He studied them as a group, then individually. They seemed to move as one with their boards and the waves as naturally as turtles in the water. *Totally amazing,* Snap thought. It was interesting to see that there were mostly turtles surfing the Pacific waters. Only every once in a while you would see an out-of-towner, like a flamingo or even a bearded dragon going out for a surf.

"Ya with me brah?" Timmy picked up his board.

"Yeah, man. I'm so ready for this."

"Calm yourself. Remember, you're on a short board now. It's different the first time out."

"I always thought a shorter board would be easier."

"I wouldn't say easier man, but it does make it possible to do tricks and have more control." Timmy smiled while leashing up.

The thruster was definitely lighter than Snap's heavy long board. Once they were both ready to go, Timmy gave one last instruction. "Okay, lets go. Shuffle your feet to warn the stingrays you're coming out."

"Stingrays?" Snap quivered.

"No worries, brah. They're cool with us. Just gotta let them know you're coming out so they won't accidentally sting you. They'll move."

Snap trusted Timmy's advice, but decided to ride out on his belly to avoid the stingers just in case. Both turtles paddled out through the first set of waves. Timmy told Snap to look down shore in order to check out the way the waves crashed.

"Let's paddle down a bit. That's a nice set over there." Timmy motioned for Snap to follow. Once they found the right spot, they duck dived into the waves, going out for the good ones.

"You ready man?"

Snap nodded.

"I want you to concentrate on the flow of your shell with the wave. Ride left to right, rail to rail." Timmy

instructed. Snap didn't waste time and got ready. When he saw his wave, he paddled forward and let the wave pick up his board as he hopped from his belly to feet, but immediately lost balance and tipped over.

"Be patient, brah. The shorter boards are made for *you* to control every movement." Timmy explained the process after Snap was sitting back on his board.

Snap swam out to try again. This time losing balance while still on his belly. "What am I doing wrong, Timmy?" he yelled.

"Taking yourself *way* too seriously brah. Watch man." Timmy turned his board and let the next wave pick him up and carry him in.

"I'll show you how goofy foots do it!" Timmy yelled.

Snap watched Timmy and then paddled out and tried once more. After the wave lifted his board, he hopped to his feet again, wobbling to the left. He was able to save his balance and stay up. He could feel the pressure of the back of the wave catching up with him, so he moved left and right parallel and with the wave. His ride was perfect, well…until Squirt arrived and tipped him over.

"Hey!" Snap yelled at the seal doing a victory flip a few feet away.

Timmy laughed and swam over to say hi to the goofy seal. "See brah, it just takes a few tries to get used to the short board." Timmy winked and patted Squirt on the head. The seal spit water into the air and went back under.

Both turtles took turns watching each other. Snap was learning so much from Timmy's style. He was so smooth when he rode. Just like a pro. Snap tried to repeat everything he witnessed his coach do. Neither of them did much talking. It was just understood what needed to be done after the basic coaching was finished. Timmy seemed to let Snap figure some things out on his own. The longer they practiced, the less Timmy talked.

First Time for Everything

Snap wiped out just as many times as he rode in. The pair took a break to lay out on the sand where Timmy explained to him it didn't matter how many perfect waves he rode, so long as each time he wiped out, he got up and did it again.

The full afternoon of surfing had definitely worn Snap out, especially after the long trip over to Pacific Beach. He had pushed himself harder in just a few days than he had all summer on the baseball field.

"You've definitely impressed me. Do you know why you're so good?" Timmy asked while they walked back to the car.

"Because I'm a goofy foot?" Snap asked.

Timmy laughed. "Yeah brah. That's it."

They continued walking toward the car when Snap finally asked, "Timmy? What's a goofy foot, anyhow?" He hoped it wasn't something bad.

Timmy explained that a goofy foot was a rider who surfed with their right foot forward, facing the wave when they're riding left along the tube.

"So, is that why it's sorta natural for me?" Snap asked.

"That's not it." He smiled. "You're different, brah." He patted Snap's head. "Come on! Seriously, don't you know why you're so good already?"

"Huh? What do you mean?" Snap had never been asked a question like that before, plus he wasn't sure if he would say he was *that* good. "I've just wanted to do this my whole life."

"It shows." That was all Timmy said about the matter. They left the beach together and made their way down to Mission Bay to meet everyone for the bonfire.

Chapter 6

The 'Oia'i'o

Mission Bay was full of animals of every species. RVs and campers lined up alongside the road, which curved around the entire bay. Families were flying kites, ducks were skiing on the back of speedboats, seals were sailing, and there were even yoga classes full of meditating turtles. Snap figured this must have been one of the family spots Tula had mentioned to him.

Snap heard someone calling to him and Timmy. "Hey, over here!" Snap spotted Tula waving under a huge tent with their friends. She had a trash bag tied to one of the tent legs, and it was overflowing with empty water bottles and paper. Snap knew Tula was a member of the local Turtle Society, and she frequently spent her free time volunteering. Today it seemed, was no different.

Herbert, Star, and Trekker were gathered around the Olive Ridley bale. Down the way, Snap caught a glimpse of the moped-riding Leatherbacks gathered around Lucas, of course.

"Did you rip it up out at Wind n' Sea, brah? I heard the waves are gnarly right now," Barney asked while picking at his shell.

"It was awesome, bro," Snap said with a somewhat tired tone.

"It's *brah*," D.J. Slide whispered. "So the surf was totally legit today or what?"

"Legit." Snap nodded.

"He was full on!" Timmy yelled from the fire pit.

"You look beat, man." Spike patted the back of Snap's shell. "Well, you'll be stoked to see the surf out in Trestles. Lowers is such a great wave. That's where you *would've* competed," Spike said.

Tula gave Spike a strange look. "What?" he asked his sister. "Dude, what's the matter with you?"

"I told you to keep your beak shut!" Tula snapped at her brother. "Unless he changed his mind with Timmy today." Tula handed her trash bag to Spike. "Your turn!"

"Whatever! I helped you all day at Pacific Beach." Spike handed the bag back to Tula. "So, seriously brah? You're not competing?"

Snap was feeling the effects of a long day on the water, and he really didn't feel like getting into this particular conversation, especially with Timmy standing within earshot. "Can we just relax for a minute?" Snap started to sit down directly where he had been standing when all of a sudden…

"Pardon me!"

Snap recognized the peculiar French accent.

"*Excusez-moi!*"

Snap looked down to see Herbert busy wiping sand away from his shell.

"Oh, sorry Herb, I didn't even see you." Snap looked closely and noticed Herbert's new shell. "I hardly recognized ya dude. Is that a new shell or what?" Snap moved over, inspecting the sand before he sat down, and plopped himself comfortably on the ground.

"Precisely *monsieur*." Herbert readjusted his shell and blew sand out of his bifocals. "Yesterday, my trusty companion here,

The 'Oia'i'o

noticed a hole in the top of my previous shell, so I traded mine in for a new one in Pacific Beach this morning."

"I'm sure Star *was* the first to notice," Snap smiled. "Since he was the one who made the hole," Snap said under his breath.

The other turtles laughed at the comment, all knowing full well Star had surely snacked on Herbert's back a few times too many.

Snap leaned over and asked Tula to confirm if starfish actually ate hermit crabs.

"Shh. Herb doesn't know that," she said.

Snap thought Herbert was a relatively intelligent crab. *He has to know,* he thought. "Well. I figured that. But maybe the starfish don't eat the crabs where Herbert is from?" Snap directed his attention back to Herbert and asked, "France, right?"

Herbert went back to his own pleasantries, spewing philosophy to anyone who would hear him as he kindly saluted Snap with a *"Oui, oui."*

"He's not French, silly. That crab was born and raised in California," Tula said.

"Then what's up with the accent?"

"Beats me. I think he tried out for a French role at Sea World and got turned down."

"I heard that! If you are referring to my accent, my mother crab was born in the south of France. She was an *ar'tist* and owned a pastry shop."

"Whatever Herb." Tula, like the others, returned to a different conversation.

Once the sun reached the horizon out in the bay, Timmy fired up the pit. Snap thought about his dad as he looked at all the families gathered together around makeshift fires. The older animals were busy talking amongst themselves, and the little ones were all gearing up for roasted marshmallows.

The turtles entertained themselves that evening playing ping-pong and throwing a frisbee until it got dark. Spike's frisbee accidentally caught the wind and flew right over Lucas' head, almost knocking off his bandana. "Score," Spike said under his breath.

"I would be careful if I were you, Spike," Tula warned her brother. "You don't know what Lucas might have up that cuff of his if you get him heated."

"What are you talking about? You talk back to him all the time."

"Yeah, but I'm a girl. He isn't going to do anything to me. She smiled and started playing with the bracelet on her wrist. "Come on, let's go sit by the fire!"

The turtles sat down together around the bonfire that was starting to crackle, and it gave off just the right heat to warm them as they sat in the cool evening breeze by the bay. They each passed the bag of marshmallows around and patiently waited for Timmy to get settled on a rock. A few of the Leatherbacks walked over with Lucas carrying fire-roasted clumpy blobs on the ends of sticks.

"What in the world is Lucas and his bale holding on their sticks?" Snap asked.

"Jellyfish. Leatherbacks like that kind of fatty meat," Tula said. "It just looks *gross* if you ask me."

A few more turtles gathered near Timmy's fire. Snap watched as Timmy waited and welcomed all the animals in. Soon everyone around the bonfire was quiet, and all that could be heard was the subtle crashing of the waves behind them and the crackling sound of burning wood. Everyone was anticipating Timmy's stories. The look on Timmy's face became serious, as he prepared to tell his legends from long ago. His eyes were wide, and his voice was powerful.

The 'Oia'i'o

He began, *"Long, long ago in a far away sea lived a green sea turtle, kinda like myself, who traveled the oceans in search of the perfect wave. On the night of a full moon, she visited a forbidden beach full of beautiful yet dangerously alluring shades of green and blue. Turtles lose themselves when surrounded by such telling colors. Emerald, sea foam green, aqua blue, jade, cobalt, and my personal favorite, jungle green. Can you picture the colors?"*

All the turtles, including Lucas and his band of troublemakers, had their mouths wide open. Snap looked over at Barney and noticed his mouth was actually watering, either that or Snap thought he was just drooling. *Dude?*

"Yes, you could almost taste the candy colors. Now beneath the beautiful Bermuda Cedar tree laid a shell with an engraved 'Oia'i'o Hawaiian symbol inside its coils. The symbol represented truth of the self, the soul, the true turtle within each of us. The inner puka."

Timmy leaned in toward the group and drew the symbol with the end of a stick in the sand, then carefully and slowly repeated the word sound by sound. "Oye-ah-eoh."

"Oye-ah-eoh," Snap and Tula repeated under their breath.

"The harmony and balance of the symbol speaks to all who have had the privilege to wear it. Harmony and balance of the soul, the body, and the mind come together in her presence. Some say if you wear this shell, you will see images of her out in the ocean on a full moon. Her cries will vibrate in your ears and feet. The sounds will paralyze you from movement. And some say, you can see her, but only in the midst of the absolute, perfect ride."

There was a familiarity in Timmy's story, and Snap began to feel a bit uncomfortable. He started toying with the shells on his necklace and turned to see Lucas watching him from outside the bale. He appeared eerie to Snap, with a dark shadow cast back behind him, his eyes glowing because of the flames in the fire pit.

"What happened to the turtle?" Lucas asked, interrupting the story. Some of the other turtles shushed him, and Tula reached across the group and pegged him with a marshmallow.

"Vanished. She fell in love with the colors my dear friends. Now, back to the shell she left behind. It is said that it's infused with gifts and was first discovered deep inside the treasures of the Hawaiian underwater volcanic home of our species. It was referred to as the heaven of turtles before the lavas transformed and exposed the caves to the outer world. They say the shell has traveled all over the world, always in search of a master, an owner worthy of wearing it. It has been seen throughout the years on every shore on the planet, at different times since the beginning of the turtle species." Timmy kept his head still, and with his eyes, he looked around at each turtle and stopped when he saw the blank stare of Snap Shell. *"And it is said, it will always be returned to the rightful owner. The discoverer must give the shell to the chosen one or they will be cursed for all eternity. An unbalanced soul is forbidden to wear such a symbol. The chosen one is the only keeper who can use its powers to defeat negative forces. But if you are not the keeper of the shell, you will reap its destruction because the spirit of the great turtle, the First, they call her, lives inside the shell."*

Snap's eyes were wide, and he could feel Lucas staring at him. He tried to tuck the necklace he was wearing into his shell.

"Totally awesome," Barney said under his breath.

Getting restless, Snap leaned back away from the group, away from the light of the fire and flames and tucked his chin over his necklace, worried that somehow someone might confuse *his* necklace for the one in the story. He inspected the symbol Timmy

The 'Oia'i'o

drew in the sand and realized his necklace had the *same* symbol. His necklace bore the 'Oia'i'o symbol just as Timmy described it.

"I totally know who Timmy's talking about," Tula whispered to Snap.

Snap looked around and leaned in closer, to conceal his necklace. "You do?"

Tula nodded yes and said, "He's totally talking about Wrinklebutt."

"What? How do you know? It's not like he even said it was her," Snap argued.

"I know Timmy's stories are real." Tula kept on.

"They're made up ghost stories, Tula. Or better yet, kinda like those ancient Greek Turtle mythologies that turn into major motion pictures. Come on." Snap tried to convince her the story wasn't true and realized he was trying to convince himself.

"Why are you acting so weird about it then?" Tula pointed out.

"It's just..." Snap dropped the subject. "I'm not. I'm just saying. It's a totally wicked story, that's all."

Soon, Timmy changed the subject and started telling other stories, tales of great turtles, scary turtles and the stories most of the local turtles have heard since they were younger. The stories continued on through the night until the moonlight lit up the ocean. As it got later, Timmy finally ended his tales, and they all cleaned up, put out the fire and prepared to head home.

That evening, Timmy dropped all the turtles off at their houses. Snap was crammed in the backseat between Barney who was snorting and drooling all over his own shell, and Tula, whose sleepy head had fallen onto Snap's shoulder. He could have done without the continual snort in one ear, but he didn't seem to mind Tula's head on his shoulder shell.

The Olive Ridleys were dropped off at little beach huts lined up along the shore. They were encamped around

each other, surrounding a larger hut that resembled a school or large gymnasium.

"Hey, look at that," Snap said, shaking Tula so she would wake up. "What are those?"

"Huh? What are whats?" She looked around, and before she understood his question, she realized how close she was cuddled next to Snap Shell.

"Did I fall asleep?"

"Yeah, on me, or well, on my shoulder."

"Oh. Sorry about that." She blushed. "What was your question again? What are what's?"

"I didn't mind." Snap looked away and back at the huts.

"Oh. Those are our houses. We all check in with the elders," she said between heavy yawns. "And we help do chores around the houses and cook, or mostly eat the food they make. Miss Webber, a retired duck, cooks for us inside the big building over there."

"It's like an orphanage then?" *Dude, probably not the right word,* Snap thought.

"No. I wouldn't call it that. More like our own village or like I always say, our resort."

Snap thought about the things Tula told him this morning about being lucky to have a parent who cares and realized *resort* may have been Tula's way of hiding that she didn't have her own parents around.

When they stopped, Tula and the others got out of Timmy's car and left Snap in the backseat by himself. "See you tomorrow. I'll show you around our huts sometime."

To try and make her feel better, Snap said, "You mean, show me around the resort."

Tula smiled and walked away.

The 'Oia'i'o

Snap rode the rest of the way, silently in the backseat. Once Timmy pulled up to Snap's house, he turned around and handed Snap a folded up napkin. "It's going to be a long week little buddy, so you need to get some rest. You may have been rippin it out there today, but Trestles' wave is going to be different. It's a *good* different, but still different."

Snap unfolded the napkin which had different days of the week written next to a surf break name.

"After class you'll be spending those days with me, getting to know waves, the break, the weather, wind, everything you need to know before the big competition."

Snap studied the napkin for a moment using the light from inside Timmy's car.

Monday-Churches (Trestles)
Wednesday-Swames (Encinitas)
Friday-Lowers (Trestles)

"Timmy, there's something I need, um, want to tell you." Snap wrestled with himself to find the right words. "What I mean is, I don't even know if I *can* compete." He said the words and looked at Timmy, hoping he wouldn't be upset with him. Having to please his father was already difficult without having to disappoint his new surf instructor.

"Do you want to surf?" The Green sea turtle asked with a raised brow.

"Well, yeah. I loved it out there today."

"Then just do it for the surf."

"Why are you going to spend all that time..."

Timmy cut him off. "I've gotta give back brah. It's the energy of life."

"Thanks then." Snap hopped out of Timmy's Camaro, almost forgetting the Sea Trek helmet and gear in the back. When he looked up at the house, he could see his dad outside reading a book on the balcony, probably one of his many science books. Mr. Shell eyed Timmy in his car and waved down to him.

"Do you want to come in?" Snap turned around to ask, but Timmy revved the engine and was already driving off. Snap knew it was time to have the talk that he had been dreading all day with his dad.

He sauntered upstairs, almost hesitating on purpose. He knew his father had already seen him standing on two feet and would ask him about it again. But, to lighten his load and not make matters worse, he resorted to the more traditional means of walking his father preferred.

"Whatcha reading Pops?" Snap sat down in the chair across from his dad, exhausted from the long day.

"Oh, just an article about the changing bay environment. I'm about to run some tests next week for my own research."

His father kept talking, but Snap cut him short. "Cool."

"How was the park?" his father asked.

Snap forgot that his dad didn't know about the plans changing to a day of surfing. "Oh, well, the other turtles went to Belmont, but Timmy took me to La Jolla to practice surfing on his short board. He's really helping me."

"For what? Competing?"

"Yeah." Snap gulped. He responded before his father could reply. "He thinks I'm really good. And I really am, Pops. You should see me out there on the water and the waves!" Snap paused to see if his father would agree before continuing. "But don't worry so much. I'm not trying to compete, even if Timmy thinks I should."

The 'Oia'i'o

"Look, son. I have my reasons for not trying to make it out on top of the ocean. It's just those bigger waves are dangerous. But I understand, you have your mother's spirit in you." His father sighed and said, "So, I guess I will have to respect that's why you love the ocean so much."

"So are you say…" Snap didn't know if that meant his dad was okay with him competing or not.

"I guess I should have known this was coming." Mr. Shell spoke up again.

"What do you mean, Pops?"

"You can surf son, just no competing." Mr. Shell had a sad look in his eyes when he said those words to his son, the same look Snap recognized when his father looked at old pictures of his mother. Mr. Shell got up from his chair, looked over at his son, nodded and left the balcony. "I understand son. You and I are just…different."

Snap watched his father disappear into the house. *Well, that went well.* He looked up at the sky and sighed, still not knowing what his father meant by all of it.

The moon was full, and the air was clear. It was getting late, and he realized how exhausted his muscles felt. Snap crawled in bed and picked up the frame on his nightstand. "Good night, mom," he said to the frame. It was times like these he wished his mom was still here. She would have let him compete, he just knew it. After he carefully placed the frame back beside him, he pulled the covers over his shell. Snap fell asleep and began to dream again.

Snap was with his dad on what looked to be a deserted island. Wrinklebutt, or a turtle he thought was Wrinklebutt, was sitting on the edge of a waterfall. Her shell, the rocks and the waterfall all formed together in the shape of a triangle. The scene fast-forwarded to Mr. Shell taking something from the big sea turtle's flipper. Snap couldn't hear a word they said in his dream, but he saw the item that was exchanged. It was the necklace, his mother's necklace he now wore around his neck. In the dream his father looked toward him and behind him, and the sea turtle disappeared into the ocean.

"We have to go save her, Pops. She came back to us, but she'll die out there."

"It's okay, son. She wasn't really there. I have her necklace."

"It's my necklace, Pops. And she is real. We have to save her or she'll never come back."

"We can't swim underwater, son. We must stay here."

"Forever?"

"Yes, forever."

"No. I can swim. I have flippers."

"No, you don't, son. You used to have flippers."

"We have to get off the island, Pops!"

Snap looked down at his feet and noticed they were changing into real flippers. "Look! It's working!" As Snap's feet started to transform, he could feel the vibration in his feet from beneath the ground. The vibration got stronger and louder, and he started to hear a loud noise that sounded like a garbage truck coming from nowhere. The ground beneath him started shaking, and he was plucked from his dream by the sound of his father's voice.

"Son, wake up! Hurry!"

"What's going on?" Snap was confused, unsure if he was still dreaming or awake.

"Son, you have to get out of bed!" He heard his father yelling. "Hurry, Snap! Hurry! Snap, come on, wake up son!"

When Snap fully opened his eyes and realized he was no longer dreaming, he panicked.

The 'Oia'i'o

"What's happening Pops?"

"Son, get out of bed!"

"Why? What's going on?" Snap noticed the books on his shelves were shaking. Some of the things in his room were falling over, and outside car alarms were going off.

"**Earthquake!** Get in the doorframe and inside your shell! **NOW!**"

Chapter 7
The Green Flash

Snap jumped quickly out of bed, startled from being awakened from his dream and unsure of what was happening. His father grabbed his son's hand and pulled him under the doorframe for safety. All around him things were falling to the ground. Snap heard the sound of glass shattering. He glanced at the floor and saw the broken picture frame. *Mom,* he thought and reached for the frame, but his dad held him back. The sound of the house shaking frightened him, so he hid his head inside his shell. Mr. Shell held him close, repeatedly asking if he was okay. A few moments later everything fell silent. Snap waited for his dad's cue to move. The earth shook the house one more time beneath his feet, and then it was over.

"Alright, son. I think it's over," his dad said.

Snap poked his head and arms out of his shell. "Are you sure?" he asked. "I don't feel very good."

His father reassured him that everything was okay as he looked around the room.

"So that's what an earthquake's like?" Snap struggled to take a step forward and reached for his father to help regain his sense of balance.

Mr. Shell helped his son over to the bed, avoiding the glass on the floor and said, "Yep. I think we're going to have more than one of those this year." Mr. Shell patted Snap on the head and gave his son a big hug around his shell.

"How bad do you think it was, Pops?"

"It's hard to tell son, but that's what the Richter Scale is for. We'll have to look it up online later." Mr. Shell adjusted his nightcap and told his son to get back into bed. "I'm going to have a look around the house before turning in for the night."

"Don't you want me to help you pick all of this stuff up?" Snap asked before getting back in bed.

"No, no. You get some rest, and I'll take care of it."

Snap knew his father was anxious by the way he continually fumbled with his nightcap, but he also knew his dad would do anything to make him feel safe.

"But that's it. Right, Pops? Everything is okay, right? What if it comes back?"

Mr. Shell was already leaving the room to get a broom when he turned to say, "I can sleep in here if you want me to, son."

Snap didn't say anything else about it. He did want his dad to stay with him, but he didn't ask, so he climbed back into bed.

Mr. Shell inspected every room in the house to make sure everything was still secure. Once he finally returned to Snap's room to check on him, he found his son drifting off. He picked up a few things that had fallen off the bookshelves and nightstand, including the frame that held a picture of his wife. Once he was finished sweeping the glass from off the floor, he grabbed a blanket from the foot of his son's bed and laid himself down on the floor next to his son.

Soon after his father laid down, Snap woke back up, still a bit shaken up by the earthquake and feeling very restless. He looked at the broken picture frame on his nightstand and reached over to pick it up, and as he did, he heard a growling sound coming from the floor.

Dude! What in the world is that? He looked down to find his dad curled up with a blanket on the floor. Snap smiled when he saw his pops next to his bed. He eased out of bed, trying not to wake his dad while adjusting the blanket on his father.

"Go back to bed, son." Mr. Shell mumbled half asleep.

Snap smiled and tip-toed over to his desk because he really wanted to check out the online news about the earthquake. He searched on his computer and found that the quake registered as a 6.2 on the Richter Scale. Snap wasn't sure what that measurement really meant, so he watched a few amateur videos of the earthquake on Turtle Tube.

His attention was swayed once he noticed he had an email. *Iggy*, he thought! Snap had completely forgotten to email Iggy and let him know they made it to California like he promised. When he opened his email account, he already had a message from his best friend from Texas. *Ugh!* He couldn't believe he forgot Iggy. Considering all the things that had happened since he arrived, he thought now was the best time to write him. He opened the message:

Snap,
How's California? We all miss you back here in Texas. It's not the same since you left. Believe it or not, I've actually been hanging out with Cooper. He's transferring to Memorial Elementary. I also found out who our new fifth grade

teacher is, Mr. Gruff, that goat down the hall from Principal Horn's office. Have you met many turtles in California? Can you surf yet? I wish I could come and visit now. Oh, guess what? My mom is having a baby! Molly just stares at the egg in its crib all day with this angry look on her face. I think she is jealous of not being the baby anymore. Ha! Well, it's late. I couldn't sleep for some reason. Gotta go to bed. I'm going swimming with Buddy, Lizibeth and Cooper in the morning.

Write back.

Iggy

Snap was both happy and sad to hear from his best friend back home. He read the email over one more time and hit *reply*.

Iggy,
Sorry I didn't email you, man. I know I promised, but I've been pretty busy. Guess what! We literally just survived an earthquake, like an hour ago. Everything is okay. The house is still standing, and I haven't seen any real damage on the news yet. Everything here is going pretty good, man. I've met a few turtle friends. This one girl, Tula... she's pretty cute, her brother, Spike, Slide, oh and a lizard named Trek. You'd like him. He wears this helmet thing and every time he talks he has to clear the fog out of it with a "Phfff" sound. He almost reminds me of that Lord Tortoise from those Turtle Wars movies! So anyway, all the turtles here surf with me, and they're trying to get me to compete. My instructor is like an ex-pro and he's spending all this extra time with me, dude. You should visit. I'll take you surfing. Tell our friends hi for me! I miss y'all, but love the beach too!

Laters,
Snap

The Green Flash

As he finished sending his email, he heard his dad's alarm clock going off. *6:00 AM*, he thought. *Right on time.* As soon as it sounded, Mr. Shell hopped up to his hands and feet, and started to groan.

"Oh, *my shell*," he said.

"Morning, Pops!"

"Hey! You're up early? What's the matter son, couldn't sleep?"

"No, not really. I just remembered to check my email, and Iggy wrote me. So, I told him about the earthquake and everything that's been happening here." Snap got up to help his father stretch out, and asked, "Do you think it would be okay if I walk down to the water, Pops?"

After a few more groans, his father told him it would be fine. "Just no surfing today, okay? Not after the quake."

"Okay, Pops. I won't." Snap wasn't going to argue with his dad, especially after last night. One day of not surfing after an earthquake was fine by him. He even walked on his hands and feet while inside the house, even though he was already getting used to being on his hind legs. He grabbed some gear for the day, including the helmet to drop off at Trekker's shop, and ran out of the house. He knew exactly where he was going when he left—the turtle huts.

The full moon was still casting light outside and slowly, off in the distance, the sunlight was preparing to rise above the horizon. Everything around him began to glow with the morning hue. He took a different route this time, passing by Starlucks Coffee Shop. The whole place was full of starfish inside, having their early morning caffeine fix. "So this is where all the sea stars are," he said to himself. He wondered what the inside of that place looked like during the earthquake. Bouncing sea stars everywhere, no doubt.

Once Snap reached the huts, he tip-toed around to find Tula to see if she was awake. After he knocked on the first hut's flap, he heard what sounded like Barney snoring inside. "Not that one." The door flap to the next hut was wide open, and when he peeked inside, he saw Spike sound asleep with blankets up to his neck and a pillow over his face. Only his spike necklace was showing. "Next," he said to himself. He peeked inside the next open hut and found Slide playing a video game. Snap asked for Tula, and Slide nodded his head in the direction of the last hut in that row. From what he could tell, it was completely empty apart from the glittery pink beads hanging from the door. *That's gotta be it,* he thought. He stuck his head through the strands of beads, but Tula was nowhere to be found.

"Tula?" he whispered. Snap didn't want anyone to think he was sneaking into her room, but he couldn't help but take a few moments to look around from the doorframe. There was a picture of Tula with her mom sitting on her nightstand and another one with Spike on her dresser.

"Hey!"

Snap spun around quickly and found Tula standing directly behind him. "Can't sleep after the quake?" she asked.

"Yeah."

"Me too," she nodded. "Bet you don't see many of those in Texas, huh?"

Snap agreed and wondered how long she had been standing there.

"I see you brought the helmet, too?" Tula giggled.

"Yeah, well...I was going to return it to the shop when it opened."

"I've got a better idea. Whenever I can't sleep, or I have something on my mind, I always go to my favorite spot in California. Wanna go?" she asked.

The Green Flash

"Where are we going?"

"O.B."

"Where?" Snap asked.

Tula told him, "Ocean Beach."

"What's there?"

"Sunset Cliffs, of course!" She smiled, immediately grabbing Snap's hand to come with her.

"Oh." He thought for a moment, then asked, "Ocean Beach? Isn't that down by Pacific Beach?"

"Yep. And we call it, P.B. You can just use the helmet!"

"Wait," he stopped there for a minute to think about it. "We're going to swim *right after* an earthquake?"

"The quake started miles and miles away in Mexico. We'll be fine! Come on!" Tula motioned for him to follow her again.

The turtles jogged down the boardwalk to Solana Beach, and Tula found the perfect spot for them to get in the water. Snap noticed there weren't many animals out that early in the morning, except a few couples taking strolls along the beach.

"Tula, are you sure this is a good idea?" Snap questioned, as Tula put her toes in the water.

"What? Are you scared? I mean, we *can* take the Coaster there if you want," she said, splashing water at him with her flipper.

"No, it's okay. I trust you. If you think it's safe. Let's go." Snap put on the helmet and asked Tula to make sure everything looked secure. He knew his pops said not to go surfing, but he never said anything about swimming.

"Come on!" Tula grabbed his hand again.

Snap let out a big breath of air and went back under into the world of fish and sea turtles. The two slowly passed through the reefs and caves of Del Mar and La Jolla. Snap recognized the area from their last underwater adventure. The seahorse stables of Del Mar were closed up and quiet this time. Snap passed the stables as Tula swam next to him and they both looked around for Suzzy. *She must be sleeping like normal animals*, he thought.

As they continued on, Snap started getting restless because he wanted to swim the rest of the way. Walking underwater took so long, and he was kinda ready to be there already. He looked above him, noticing the waters seemed unusually rough up on the surface as they walked further and further, which brought back some of his anxiety. He figured swimming would make the trip faster, and considered taking off his helmet. It couldn't be that hard to hold his breath under water. If Tula could do it the whole way, he could surely manage with a few breaks in between. Snap took one huge gulp of air from inside the helmet and shimmied out of his gear. For the first time he felt the cool water on his face. He opened his eyes and paddled his back feet as hard as he could and swam up to Tula's side. She nearly choked when she saw him without the helmet.

"Snap! Your helmet!" Bubbles flew out of her mouth. Tula looked back and saw the Sea Trek helmet sitting on the ocean floor. All sorts of small fish and sea urchins had already started gathering around the contraption as if they found a new spot to call home.

Snap smiled and motioned to her it was okay. She asked him if he was sure he knew what he was doing, and he nodded, yes. He didn't want to risk swallowing water by opening his mouth to answer her. The pair swam together, with Snap holding his breath the entire way. When they reached the waters of Pacific Beach and Mission Bay, Tula came up to let him take a breath.

"I can't believe you took off the helmet! Aren't you full of surprises?"

Snap gave her a nod and took in a deep breath of air, realizing that he would have to find a way to return the helmet to Trekker at some point. "Whatever we do, I can't forget the helmet," he said.

"Yeah, Trek would *not* be happy. Have you ever seen an angry lizard? They do weird things with their tail!"

"Ha!" Snap pictured, Iggy, who hardly ever got angry, and his long clumsy tail.

"We can just get it on the way back," she reassured. "Ready to keep going? We're almost there."

"Let's do it, dude." Snap took in his final gulp of air, and both turtles went back under. After a ten-minute stretch, they finally reached the Ocean Beach Pier.

Tula and Snap swam some more and took another short break for air. "We're almost there! You can see the cliffs from here," Tula said.

Snap's eyes grew wide. "Wow. They're…they're…huge!" Snap was starting to feel disoriented after being under water and holding his breath for so long. Tula noticed and asked if he was okay.

"I think so. Is there a snack stand or something in Ocean Beach? I'm starving!"

"Snack stand? At the cliffs? It's about time you became a little less high maintenance and grab yourself a handful of kelp and seaweed before you pass out." Tula disappeared under the water for a moment, and when she returned, she pulled out a handful of green slime in her flipper and stuffed it in her mouth. She finished with a loud slurp. "It's like eating spinach."

"This slime does *not* look like spinach to me!" Snap said with a disgusted look on his face.

"It's great for digestion. Come on, it's like three hundred percent of your daily fiber." Tula handed Snap a giant ball of seaweed.

"Ya see," he paused and hesitated to eat the *vegetable*, "it's more of a texture thing." He argued a few more points before she insisted.

"Just eat it! You're such a girl!"

"*What?*" Snap couldn't believe a girl was calling him a girl. "Fine!" Snap covered his nose holes with two of his fingers and stuffed the wad of slime in his open mouth.

"Swallow. Don't just hold it in your mouth, silly! That looks gross."

Snap gulped down the seaweed so he would have the energy to make it through the rest of the day. A turtle's got to do what a turtle's got to do.

"See, that wasn't so bad."

"If you like the taste of salt water!" Snap shivered.

"Whatever. Let's get to the cliffs to see who's out there surfing after the quake."

"Surfing? Who would surf right after an earthquake?" Snap said. The waters almost seemed too rough for swimming.

The turtles waded up to the shore before reaching the cliffs to avoid getting smashed against the rock walls. They arrived at a set of stone steps leading up to the top of one of the cliffs. Snap followed Tula all the way up.

"Why is this place called Sunset Cliffs, anyway?" Snap asked once they reached the top.

"You'll see later!" Tula smiled and pulled an identical, but dry swim skirt out of her shell. "Turn around, and no peeking."

"Huh?"

"My skirt," Tula said, waving it in his face. "This one is cold and wet!" She tugged at the skirt she was wearing.

"Oh, sorry." Snap blushed and turned to focus on a nearby stone. "The cliffs are huge, huh?"

"I said, *no peeking*!"

"I'm not. Why don't you go do that in a cave or something?"

"Not you! Gill. I can see him peeking from behind that rock. Nosey!" Tula yelled.

Snap turned and spotted Gill who was sitting on a higher ledge.

"Hey, I'm not finished!"

"You're just tying your bow!" Snap huffed and looked back up at Gill.

Tula started to walk out to the lookout point. "Look! There's Herbert and Star. They're down there with Timmy."

"Timmy's down there?"

"Of course. We had a totally awesome quake this morning, and Timmy lives for a good challenge."

Snap shook his head in amazement. *Who would surf only a few hours after an earthquake*? The more Snap learned about Timmy, the more extreme he seemed. But then again, Snap actually swam from Cardiff all the way to O.B. after an earthquake too.

Both turtles watched as Timmy started rock climbing up the other side of the cliff, obviously trying to get to the highest jumping point. Herbert looked up and spotted the turtles, and climbed up their side of the cliff to join them.

"Hey, Herb. Doing some cliff diving?" Tula asked.

"Precisely, madam."

"I thought you were afraid of heights."

"Did I say that?" Herbert asked, tapping one claw to his mouth. "Oh, I was just being modest."

"Look, there he goes." Tula pointed at Timmy who was at one of the highest points on Sunset Cliffs. Timmy held both hands over his head, and without hesitation, dived into the ocean beneath him. He barely made a sound when hitting the water. The waves thrashed over the spot that took him under.

"Wow! That was amazing." Snap stood in awe and waited for Timmy's head to pop up out of the water. Once Timmy popped up, he swam over to grab his board from off the bottom ledge.

Herb brought the attention back to himself, naturally. "Should I jump, Star?"

Star shook his head no.

"You're exactly right. I *should* just jump." Herbert left the turtles to climb down the cliff with Star stuck to his back until he was only an inch from the water. He jumped, flailing and screaming during the half second he was in the air.

"Doesn't he know how to swim?" Snap asked.

"Drama." Tula shook her head.

The turtles watched Timmy surf and do his morning workouts till high noon. After lunchtime, which consisted of more kelp and seaweed, they explored the caves and passages within the cliffs. Snap met a family of lobsters, who had lived at the cliffs for years, an old starfish the size of a basketball, claiming he was a fortune teller, and a sea urchin who talked entirely too much to anyone who would listen. Snap figured he was over-exaggerating most of his adventures, but the sea urchin was quite a sight. *It's hard to trust something with no face,* Snap thought.

The afternoon led into the early evening and the arrival of a surprise visitor. Tula jumped to a tap on her shoulder. "Spike!? You're here?"

"Surprised to see me?"

Snap noticed his foot flipper tapping the ground.

"Well, kinda." She shrugged.

Snap suddenly felt awkward like they had done something wrong the way Spike kept tapping his flipper.

"I was worried. You usually tell me where you're going. You've been gone all day." Spike scolded his sister.

Tula gave her brother an annoyed look and said, "Spike, I'm like eleven years old now."

"Yeah, well that's not that old."

Spike being a 13 year-old teenager now, was trying to act like a responsible big brother and watch out for Tula. *It must be a teenager thing,* Snap thought.

"Snap's been with me the whole time."

Spike looked over at Tula's new buddy and rolled his eyes. "Of course."

Snap thought it was weird to hear them argue about her being alone, considering they *all* seemed to be on their own in the huts. He knew Sunset Cliffs was her favorite spot by the way she talked about it, and apparently, by what she and Spike discussed, it wasn't everyday that she brought someone with her to *her* spot. Noticing Spike's expression, Snap got a little worried and gave the older Olive Ridley an "it wasn't my idea" look.

"It's just that it's my responsibility to..."

Tula cut him off. "You used to be so laid-back. I wasn't swimming to Hawaii. I was at the cliffs all day. I'm always at the cliffs, and you know that!"

"Actually, *we're* always at the cliffs," Spike added.

Tula had failed to tell Snap that even though she spent hours on the cliffs looking out into the ocean when she was lonely, or worse, when she missed her mom, she didn't do it alone. It was sacred time for the Olive Ridley and a special place for both siblings.

"Spike, it's not a big deal, really," Tula said.

"Fine." Spike walked down to the lower edge and sat facing the direction of the sunset by himself, not saying another word.

Snap wasn't sure how to react. On the one hand, he was enjoying the new experience with Tula but on the other hand, he felt bad for having come between the brother and sister.

"I don't know what crawled up his shell," Tula said. "He never acts like that. *Ever*!"

Snap thought about all the times he spent alone, isolated away from his pops, thinking about his mother. He knew and understood how much it hurt to miss someone you love. "I think I know why Spike's upset." Snap tried to come up with a way of explaining to Tula that it probably wasn't because she was at the cliffs all day, but because she wasn't with Spike at the cliffs.

"No, Snap. He's just being over-protective."

Snap tried to offer some advice, "Well, from what you…"

She cut him off. "Look, it's really none of your business. I think I can handle my own brother just fine."

Snap was trying to explain something to her at the same time she was talking and was only able to say, "…maybe he sees me as a threat?"

Tula laughed. "A threat? Who would be threatened by a box shell turtle?"

"Oh, forget it." Snap moved over and stood by himself, looking over at her brother.

"Sorry, that was rude." Tula bit her lip. "Please don't pout. Come sit with me. I don't want to argue." She dusted off a spot on a rock to sit.

Snap was still feeling defensive about being called a box shell turtle. Like it was a bad thing to be a box shell. "Fine." He sat down anyway. *Girls,* he thought.

"Have you ever seen a California sunset?" Tula completely changed her tone.

The Green Flash

Snap continued to stare out toward the horizon, the rolling waves that formed the life force of all turtles, and in awe of the moment he said, "No, not like this."

"Like what?" she questioned.

"Um, *with* someone." Since arriving in California, Snap had spent each evening watching the sunset, either in the background with his new friends or alone on his balcony.

The pair sat in silence as the sun slowly reached the horizon. Snap thought about his pops at home alone, his friends, Iggy and Lizibeth back home in Texas, and of course, his mom. He looked over at Tula and couldn't help but smile. "This is the most beautiful picture I've ever seen."

Tula smiled at him, turned back to face the sunset, then turned to punch him in the arm.

"What was *that* for?"

The moment was interrupted when Snap noticed Tula's brother staring at them.

Tula grabbed Snap by the shoulder. "Here it comes!" she said. "Don't blink!"

Snap was reminded of a moment in time when his mom used to say the same words.

"THE GREEN FLASH!" They both shouted at the same time.

"Wait, you saw it too?" Tula gasped.

"Well yeah," Snap started. "Well, I think I saw it. I've never seen one before now."

"Me neither. I always wait for it, but I blink or miss it somehow every time."

"That was *so* totally awesome!" Snap smiled. "I heard that whenever you see a green flash as the sun sets, it means someone's soul came back to life." Snap scratched the top of his head. "Or something like that."

Tula laughed. "Dude, that's an old turtle's tale. Look who's getting all mythological."

"I'm just saying. I saw something about it on Turtle Tube."

"You can't believe everything on Turtle Tube, dude!" She laughed.

Snap ignored her comment and pointed out the color change in front of them. "Wow, the sky just turned pink!"

"I know. This is my favorite part, it will be yellow, then orange soon." Tula leaned in and lightly nudged Snap's shoulder and his entire body tensed up.

"Romantic isn't it?" A corny French accent interrupted the moment. The pair looked down to see Herbert sitting comfortably between them.

"Herbert!" they screamed.

"*Je suis désolé*! I am sorry, my friends, did I interrupt a *moment*? Eh?"

"Moment?" Tula asked with a disgusted look. "What moment?"

Spike got up and came trailing up behind them and said, "Yeah, what moment?"

"No moment," Tula said. "Everyone, chill. And Spike, stop being such a Loggerhead!"

"What? How am I being a Loggerhead?"

"By *not* minding your own business!"

"Well, it's not my fault you've been acting different since ..."

"Since what?" Tula yelled. "Say it! I dare you to say it. Since what? Since Snap showed up?" She got up and stomped away.

Herbert clapped his claws together. "Ah, the drama! How romantic."

Spike told Herbert to *shut it,* and Snap got up to leave. "Yeah, it's probably time to go. I have a double surf at Trestles with Timmy tomorrow." Snap hopped up and followed Tula down the steps, unsure of what just happened. He looked back at Spike, hoping he would follow because he didn't know how to get back home by himself in the dark, and he wasn't sure Tula would even speak to him. "You're coming right, Spike?"

"Yeah, I'm coming," Spike said and continued to mumble, "she never sticks to her own kind."

"What did you say?" Snap wasn't absolutely sure he heard what Spike just said, but was pretty confident the comment had something to do with Tula spending time with *his kind*.

Spike brushed past Snap Shell and said, "Nothing," under his breath.

An unpleasant silence followed all the turtles as they made their way down to the shoreline. Snap, Tula, Spike, and of course, Herbert and his trusty companion, followed each other through the dark waters back to Cardiff Beach. Since no one was speaking to anyone, Snap had to schedule his own breath breaks and catch up to the group as they continued at a steady pace. Snap had never seen Tula act this way before. It was obvious to him that the comments really upset her. Each time they ventured into the ocean, she was there to check on him, always looking back to see if he was okay, but tonight, it was different. Snap felt a chill run through his shell as they passed a group of eels slithering in and out of their rocks on the swim home. He did everything he could to keep up with the group. Map or no map, this was not a place for him to get left behind.

Good for Nothing Gill

Surf Barrel 39 became the talk of the town. It was the biggest yearly event for surfing turtles and surf fans in Southern California. Word got out quickly that Snap Shell, *the box shell turtle from Texas,* had been training with the great Timmy Turtle. There was always a crowd around to cheer him on or gossip and talk about the box shell turtle during his private lessons out at Trestles. All kinds of turtles started coming to him for advice, considering he was getting firsthand lessons and instruction from the area's greatest surfer. This news didn't sit too well with Lucas, once he got wind of the box shell's newfound fame.

Over the next two weeks, Timmy's surf class started to fill up with more and more turtles wanting to learn how to master the big blue. The Hawksbill sea turtles had suddenly become interested in lessons and taking up all of Snap's spare time after class, quizzing him. One day after surf school, Tula asked Snap if he wanted to go hang out at the cliffs, but she got pushed to the side when Harry the Hawksbill insisted on talking to Snap.

"Dude. How did you get Timmy to coach you? What does it take, man? You should come hang with me and my friends at the yogurt shop tonight." The big Hawksbill turtle spoke so quickly that Snap could barely keep up.

"Why?" Tula asked from behind them. "It's not like he's even competing, Harry!" She pushed and shoved her way back up to the front of the group with Snap.

"Yeah, right!" Harry leaned in toward Snap, "Dude. Seriously. Stop hanging with the skaters. They're lame."

Tula butted in, "Don't even act like the Hawksbills don't ride skateboards, Harry!"

Harry huffed in Tula's face and turned back to Snap. "See you at the yogurt shop at seven!"

Tula looked at Snap, rolled her eyes, and walked away.

"Tula, wait up! I want to talk to you." He tried to follow her, but she quickly moved away from him. "Hey, dude, come on. What's your problem?"

"You!" She kept moving without looking back.

"Can't we just...?" Snap knew he didn't have that much time before his private lesson with Timmy, so there was no use going after her if she was in one of her moods. Spike followed after his sister and looked back, giving Snap the stink eye.

After Snap's lesson that afternoon, Timmy gave him a few follow-up pointers and told him to get some rest. "You need to learn how to conserve your energy, little man." Timmy smiled and patted Snap on the shell.

"For what...competing?" Snap questioned whether to see if Timmy would still try to convince him to compete.

"Look, brah. I know you are having doubts about competing, and it is your decision..."

"No, Timmy. It's not *my* decision. That's what everyone doesn't get. I'm a box shell. I'm a small land turtle who only a few months ago was pretending to be a surfer back in Texas. I have a parent

Good for Nothing Gill

who tells me what to do. I'm not like the sea turtles that live in huts and answer to the elders and surf animals like you. I don't get to just do whatever I want. I have an over-protective dad. It's *his* decision whether I surf or not, not mine." Snap's body started to shake with anger. For the first time in his life, he wished he were somewhere else, or worse, maybe someone else. A sea turtle.

"Look," Timmy started, "I understand. I'm not telling you to go against your pops." Timmy turned away and left Snap to his own thoughts.

"But that's what it feels like, Tim!" Snap tried to yell, but the words would barely come out. The pressure was starting to get to him, and even though he loved the attention, the waves, and being a part of something bigger than himself, the thought of disappointing his father was starting to take its toll. *What am I supposed to do?* He contemplated. He wanted to talk to his dad about it again, but that night when he got home, Mr. Shell was consumed in his work, so Snap just let it go.

The following morning, every muscle inside of Snap's shell was sore. Even his three-inch tail was sore, which was crazy. *How in the world can a tail be sore?* At breakfast, Snap toyed with the idea of bringing up the competition to his dad again. He thought about all the reasons why he wanted to surf in the competition, and jotted them down on his napkin.

He had never practiced so hard at something before in his life. This wasn't like baseball or the summer all-star league back in Texas. This was different. Baseball had been a game, a really important game, but still just a game. Surfing had become something greater. Competing in Surf Barrel was like competing in life. It wasn't just for fun. It was more, and he was really good at it. Even though he knew everything about surfing went against who he was, he felt as though he was born to do it.

His pops walked into the kitchen and started collecting berries in a bowl for breakfast. "Well, here it goes," he said under his breath.

His father glanced at the napkin of notes Snap had written and asked, "What's that, son?" Mr. Shell set down his bowl and a stack of newspapers on the table and started sifting through the pages of the most recent copy of *The Daily Shell*.

"Just needed to talk to you, if you're not too busy."

"Breakfast time is my favorite time to talk," Mr. Shell said, popping a few blueberries into his mouth.

And the only time, Snap thought. "Well, Pops, it's about Surf Barrel 39. The competition I mentioned before."

"The surf competition? I thought we already buried this discussion."

"You don't get it, Pops, all of the sea turtles are expecting me to compete. I'm good. Timmy's training me." Snap picked up his napkin of notes and started to read from his list when his father slammed his hand on the table.

"Well, STOP TRAINING WITH TIMMY!"

Snap felt his eyes swelling with tears, but he stood his ground. He needed to share his feelings with his father, even though he knew it would only upset him more. "Don't you understand? Every turtle in Turtle Town wants to train with Timmy, and he picked me! Of all the turtles he could work with, he picked me! Why can't you understand, Pops?" Snap started to feel heat rising from within him. "I'm good at it! It's almost natural to me, like I was born to do it! Why can't you just support me?"

Good for Nothing Gill

Mr. Shell looked at his son, stared right into his eyes and said, "Because it's dangerous. And because I'm your father! End of story." His father grabbed the entire stack of newspapers from the table and tucked them between his arm and shell while knocking over his glass of orange juice. He left the juice to spill over onto the floor and exited the kitchen.

Snap watched the juice as it trickled over the edge of the table. He couldn't think of anything else to say, and he didn't know what to do. Each drop of juice echoed in his mind. He shoved away his bowl of cereal, stormed out the door and headed straight to the beach.

When Snap reached the beach, he noticed Lucas with a few Leatherbacks down by the surf shop. Lucas had just gotten back from a trip to Mavericks in northern California to surf with his cousins. Snap knew that Mavericks had a killer wave and only the experienced surfers ever dared to surf those waters. A part of him was jealous, worried that he had to practice more to prove he was better than Lucas, and another part of him felt like it didn't matter. He wouldn't be surfing in the competition this summer, anyway.

Snap noticed Lucas and the other big Leatherbacks glaring at him. They immediately started talking as he passed them to get to the surf school. Little did Snap know, rumors and gossip were floating around the beach about *how* he was able to surf so well, and the rumors had nothing to do with his private lessons with Timmy. Lucas' entire bale of Leatherbacks kept the gossip flying high, even while Lucas was away.

At surf school that morning, Snap felt major tension in the air. Harry ignored him when he walked up, which Snap figured had to do with him not showing up at the yogurt shop the night before. Tula did everything she could to make sure he realized she was intentionally ignoring him too.

Trekker scolded him for leaving his helmet underwater and insisted he sweep the shop for a week to pay for any potential damage, even after Snap argued that nothing had actually *happened* to the helmet. He had a pretty good guess who told on him.

After class, Snap decided to go lay out on the beach and soak up the West Coast sun. He needed to de-stress and really just wanted to be alone. Just as he started to get comfortable Herbert and Star appeared. The hermit crab was sporting another new shell, purple this time, and Star had his customary cup of coffee.

"*Bonjour*!"

"Hey, Herb. Nice look. I do think purple is your color."

"Thanks. This one was on sale at half off. What a steal, wouldn't you say?" Herbert used a piece of cloth to dust the shell and then used it again to clean the lenses of his glasses. "Purple, they say, is the color of regalia. The color of royalty. There are volumes of recorded history where our most profound and royal crabs were known to adorn themselves in purple shells."

Snap wanted to tell Herbert that *he got what he paid for* but he didn't have the heart. "Yeah, it's great, Herb."

"Speaking of color, *monsieur*, you are looking a tad shade of blue today. Girl problems?"

"Huh? No. I'm just...I'm just..."

"Depressed? Oh, I understand." Herbert put his claw on Snap's shoulder.

"What are you talking about?"

"Star here suffers from anxiety. I am basically his counselor."

Good for Nothing Gill

Snap watched as Star shook his head again. "Maybe he just drinks too much coffee," Snap suggested. "And I'm not depressed."

"Ah, of course, of course," Herbert said. He adjusted his spectacles, studied Snap a bit more, and said, "Then it's definitely girl problems. You could always get her a shell ring down at the stand. Or wait, better yet, a pearl. I do believe they are half off today. Or was it 25 percent off? I can't quite remember."

"I'm not buying Tula a ring!" Snap looked around after he realized he was yelling.

"*Mais oui*. Of course, of course." Herbert clapped his claws together and said, "I knew Tula was the girl."

"What, no. There's nothing going on, and *we* are just fine."

"Yes, you need something of more sentimental value, I believe, *monsieur*. Why not give her your shell necklace. Or better yet. I could deliver it for you. P-r-r-ompt service, at your service!"

"What? My necklace? No way. It was my mom's. No one is getting my necklace. Especially not Tula!"

"Oh, so it was passed down?"

"Yeah, why do you care?"

"A family heirloom, no doubt."

"A family gift that is staying in my family," Snap said.

"I suppose she will just have to wait until the wedding."

"Wedding? No one is getting married, Herb. That's enough, dude!"

In the heat of the discussion, neither Snap nor Herbert noticed Gill the seagull flying overhead. The only one who did notice was Star, but being that he couldn't speak, only tap, everyone ignored him. He tried to get Herbert's attention, but the hermit crab blew him off.

"R-r-r-r. Fine! Turtles, you are all so very stubborn."

Snap was confused. "What? You just rolled your R's, and there are no R's in the word *fine*."

Herbert folded his claws. "The French roll their R's when they are angry."

"No, Herb! That's Spanish!" Snap was beginning to get a headache. He rubbed his eyes and said, "Why do you hang around us, then?"

"I hang around Timmy, to get information...for *your* information. Knowledge is power. You two love-turtles just happen to be there when I am with him. He's not just a turtle, he's *the* turtle. It's all about who you know in this world. We must network to stay on top of the vast ocean of information. No pun intended." Herbert readjusted his prescription goggles to get a better look inside the middle shell of Snap's necklace.

"Information?" Snap asked.

"Aha! So it is true," Herbert said, inspecting Snap's necklace.

"What's true?"

"Oh, nothing." Herbert pulled out a small pencil and a notepad and jotted some notes.

"Well if it's nothing, dude, can I lay out now? In peace?"

"Oh, yes of course, of course. Take a nap. Do what you like." Herbert didn't move.

Snap cleared his throat. "Can I have some privacy?"

"I'm not leaving until you tell us what's wrong."

"Fine! If you promise to go after I tell you." Snap bargained.

"You have our word." Herbert spoke for himself and Star.

"Maybe I'm a little upset that Tula has been ignoring me all week. There. Happy?"

"She's a female, *monsieur*. That's normal for girls her age." Star nodded in agreement with Herbert, and then the hermit crab added, "Actually, that's normal for all girls, no matter what age." The hermit crab finished with a *Hmm* as though he surprised himself with that information.

"I know, I know. But really, I'm *more* worried that everyone thinks I'm actually entering the surf competition."

"But aren't you, *monsieur*? It's all over The Daily Shell."

"What?"

"Yes, I wrote an article about the predicted outcome of the main surfing competitors in the paper. It's quite catchy, to pat my own shell. *Flipper to Flipper: Land vs. Sea, two turtles battle to see who claims the rights to call themselves the Surfing Champion.*"

"What? You work for the paper now? You wrote an article?"

"I have many careers. Assistant to the stars. Well, Star is my assistant, but you know what I mean. I write, I act, I am quite the natural at marketing. Oh, and I sing. Would you like to hear my demonstration? I think I could carry quite the tune for a wedding, if you get what I mean."

"No, Herb. Why would you write about something that isn't true?"

"So animals will read it, of course. What I make up is much more interesting than what really happens."

"Herbert, this isn't Hollywood. You would fit in better in L.A.."

"Oh, my dear boy, been there, done that," Herbert chuckled.

"Seriously, dude. Give me a break," Snap said.

"Well, what shall I tell the paper next?"

"Nothing! You tell them nothing!" Snap thought about it for a moment and demanded Herbert write a new story telling everyone he is not competing.

"Fine. I know exactly what the reason is behind your lack of interest in competing, *and* I know why you wear that shell necklace! Good day, sir!" Herbert tip-toed away hurriedly, with Star stuck to his new purple shell. Before the pair disappeared, Star tried one last time to point one limb up toward the sky to draw Snap's attention upward, but it didn't work.

"Wait! Why would you say that?" Snap sighed and ran over to the newspaper stand on the sidewalk. Sure enough, page five, there he was. *My shell looks kinda wide,* he thought to himself. He pictured tomorrow's headline: *"Box Shell gives up."*

Maybe Tula was right, he thought. *You can't trust anyone around here.* Snap walked back down to the beach and laid his tired body out in the sand, trying to collect his thoughts, unsure what to think about the entire situation. He closed his eyes and tried to get some rest.

As Snap was napping, Gill flew down and landed a few feet away from him. The seagull moved in closer, bouncing a few paces forward, then a few paces backward, each time easing closer and closer to Snap Shell. Gill bobbed his head left and right and finally took a snap at Snap's neck. Snap felt the tug of his necklace. When Snap opened his eyes, he saw Gill standing on him, his necklace in the seagull's beak. "Let go!"

Gill began to pull harder and harder and feeling the pressure on the back of his neck, Snap tried to shoo him away. As he did, he felt a slight tug, and the necklace was free. Before he could react, Gill was flying away with it.

"Hey! Wait! Stop! That's my mom's necklace!" Snap yelled and reached for the bird as it swooped into the air, but it was pointless. The seagull was too far out of reach.

Suddenly, another seagull, who looked just like Gill, but with much cleaner feathers and larger in size, plowed straight into the thief and snatched the necklace from Gill's beak. The pair of birds wrestled with the necklace midair, as though they were fighting for scraps of food, and before he knew it, the larger bird carried it off, heading south. *It's gone.*

Snap couldn't think of anything to do but find Tula. He went to the huts to look for her. He yelled her name over and over

Good for Nothing Gill

again until someone told him she was up at the snow cone stand with Spike.

Snap quickly ran to the stand, huffing and puffing in desperation. "Tula!"

"Snap! What happened?" She may have been upset with him, but seeing him so frantic lessened her own concerns. "What's going on?"

Snap looked at Spike, back at Tula, then at the old walrus behind the stand, and back at Tula, hesitating to talk.

"What? You can say anything in front of Spike that you can say in front of me."

Snap wasn't so sure about that anymore, but he had no choice. This was an emergency.

"Fill... I mean, Gill, the seagull..."

"The gull?" What did he do?" She noticed Snap touching his neck and said, "Wait! Where's your necklace?"

"Gill!"

"Gill has it?" Tula questioned.

"No, not Gill. I mean yes, Gill took it, but another seagull took it from him!" Snap yelled.

Tula asked him which way the birds went and said, "Gill, that pesky thief. That means *you know who* has it now."

Snap shook his head trying to catch his breath. "Who? Who?"

"LUCAS!" Tula and Spike both yelled at the same time.

"Why would he have *my* necklace?" Snap was so puzzled and exhausted from the run.

"Everyone knows Gill is a secret spy for Lucas," Spike said. "Lucas may look dumb, but he actually speaks many languages, including the language of the gull—*Squawkery*!"

Snap thought about what Spike said for a moment. How else would Lucas know everything that's going on around the beach? He's always showing up just at the right time.

"Believe us, it's him. And..." Spike paused and looked at his sister. Snap waited, and Spike said, "And there *is* the *rumor*."

"What? What rumor?" Snap perked up. *That's what Herb was mentioning,* he thought.

Spike couldn't believe Snap hadn't heard, and Tula interrupted. "Of course he wouldn't know, Spike, since it's about him."

"*Me*?"

"Where did you say you got that necklace again?" Spike asked with a raised eyebrow.

"My mom. How many times do I have to tell everyone that?"

"But where did your mom get it, Snap?" Tula said sternly.

"How would I know?"

Tula told Snap to sit down and handed him her snow cone to help cool him off. "Listen," she started, "everyone thinks you or your mom or whoever, took it from Wrinklebutt. They think the necklace is magic, Snap. It has the *Oia'i'o* symbol, and Lucas knows it. You're a threat to his record, especially now that you're training with Timmy. And since you seem to surf so great for a land turtle, well, how else would you surf like you do unless you had some magical help?"

"What? I'm not even trying to compete against Lucas. This whole barrel competition has *nothing* to do with Lucas."

"That's not what he thinks," Tula said.

"That's not what *anyone* thinks," Spike added.

Snap paused and started to think. "So all of you think the only reason why I can surf is because of my necklace?"

"Well, it's possible. Maybe you just don't know it," Tula said.

"That's just crazy, dude! Now you're accusing my mom of taking the necklace!" Snap looked at Tula and said, "My dead mom, in case you've forgotten." Snap handed the snow cone back to Tula. "I have to find Lucas."

"You can't do that, Snap!" Tula gasped.

"What's the big deal? He doesn't scare me."

"Snap. Lucas will fight you!" Spike warned.

"Whatever! I have Timmy on my side!" Snap stormed away to find Lucas down at the reef. He turned to yell at the brother and sister as he stormed away. "You're just as bad as the birds!" Snap was so fed up with all the rumors and gossip on the beach. It was starting to ruin his life. His new friends were talking about him behind his back, Lucas was bullying him, and now, the seagulls stole his mom's necklace. He had to find answers, and he wanted them now.

Snap stomped down the beach, straight into Cardiff Reef... Leatherback territory.

When he reached the reef, he found Lucas coming out of the water with his board in his flippers and his bale following behind him.

"Well, well. Look who's all-alone. Did your so-called Olive Ridley friends turn their shells on you? Who would blame them? You are a B.T.," Lucas said, inviting his friends to join in the laughs.

"Shut your mouth, Lucas. Give me back my mom's necklace."

"Oh, so you came to fight. Unfortunately, I don't have your stupid necklace, thanks to Gill."

"What's that supposed to mean?"

"It means I *should* have your necklace, which *isn't* yours by the way, but thanks to that good for nothing

Gill, it's been stolen again, this time by another seagull. Looks like you'll have to surf without it and show your true talent now—which is zero!" Lucas leaned in closer to Snap and said, "Oh wait, that's right. Rumor has it you're too chicken, or should I say too *tortoise* to compete." He laughed at his own joke.

"You mean to tell me you don't have my necklace?"

"Did you not hear me? NO! I don't! Now get out of my territory before I get mad."

Snap became angry. "I don't need the necklace to beat you, Lucas. I've seen you surf."

"Not so fast, B.T. Was that a challenge?" Lucas dropped his board to make a charge for Snap when suddenly the Leatherback stepped

right on a jellyfish. "OUCH!" Lucas started hopping on one foot. "What is my lunch doing on the ground? GILL!!! Quick, someone pee on my foot!"

"What?" his bale questioned the odd request. Each of the turtles started to look away, scratching their heads.

"Do it!!!" He hollered. "It will stop the pain!" He continued to hop up and down moaning in pain.

"No way! That doesn't really work," one Leatherback argued. "Not me," said another. Another one said, "I think I hear my mom calling," and immediately another said, "Your mom? We're sea turtles!" As that sea turtle turned to walk away, he said, "Well, *someone's* mom is calling me! I'm outta here!"

Snap scurried away before he had a chance to see who the lucky turtle would be to pee on Lucas' foot. He may have stood up to the Leatherback, but now he had a bigger problem. If Lucas didn't steal the necklace, he had to figure out who did. He ran away from the reef and immediately started to feel sick to his stomach. He began to question everything about himself, his ability to surf, his talent, his desire to become a surfer, and of course, his so-called friends. As he started to make his way home, knowing there was no way he could locate one solitary seagull amongst thousands of them, he remembered his pops. *What's he going to say about the necklace?*

CHAPTER 9
Snap Faces His Inner Cave

Sure enough, Mr. Shell noticed his son's bare neck at breakfast the next day and asked why he wasn't wearing his favorite necklace.

"Herbert's shining my shells down at the surf shop, Pops." Snap didn't want to have to explain the real story to his father yet. He needed another day to keep looking.

"Herbert? Isn't that the crab who thinks he's French?"

"Well, yeah..."

"Are you sure you can trust him with your mother's necklace, son?"

Snap knew he needed to leave the house before his lie got bigger. "I'll go get it...right now." Snap jumped out of his chair to avoid more questions. He felt horrible that he lied to his dad.

Snap was on edge all morning and avoided everyone when he got to the surf school. He had never lied to his dad before, and if that wasn't bad enough, class proved to be even worse when he could barely get up on his board. All he wanted to do was quit for the day. Everything was really starting to get to him. Lucas' evil glares toward him didn't help matters either. He was surprised to even see Lucas show up for class wearing a bandage on his foot flipper. He probably came to class just to watch Snap surf without his rumored "magical necklace."

The more he thought about everything, the more he felt everyone else might have been right. What if the necklace really did give him talent and power to conquer a skill that a box shell turtle shouldn't be able to do? What if that's why he was able to surf so easily? He questioned why his mother would have given him a gift that would only become a curse. What business did a box shell turtle from Texas have swimming, much less surfing in the ocean?

Snap noticed Timmy kept watching him during class, and afterward his instructor came over to speak to him.

"What's going on, little brah? You're all in your head today instead of in the water. What's up with that?"

Even though Snap really wanted someone to talk to, he blew him off. "It's just a bad day."

"Well dude, we all get bummed out from time to time. What's going on?"

"Nothing."

Timmy gave him a look, and Snap caved in and started telling Timmy everything.

"I lost my puka shell necklace yesterday."

"The one your mom gave you?" Timmy asked.

Snap nodded his head. "Actually, it was stolen."

"Ah, man, I'm sorry brah."

"It has the *Oia'i'o* symbol, Timmy. Everyone wants it. I'm like a walking cash register."

"Brah, are you talking about the story I told? That was just a legend. I tell stories like that all the time."

Snap Faces His Inner Cave

"I don't know, Timmy. It sounds to me like everyone believes your stories." Snap kicked his foot in the sand, accidently kicking Herbert and launching him across the beach.

"Dude. No need to take it out on the crab." Timmy tried not to laugh.

"Sorry, Herb." Snap tried to sound sincere, but Herbert wasn't exactly buying it.

"I think I'm going to walk down to the cove to clear my head."

"Good thinking. Go meditate or something. I'm sure it will come up sooner or later."

Snap walked toward La Jolla Cove. Each time he saw a seagull, his blood boiled. After yesterday, it seemed like every seagull he saw was following him. "What do you want from me? I don't have any food, and you already stole my necklace! Shoo!"

Feeling a bit paranoid, Snap felt like the seagull flying behind him looked a bit familiar. *They all look the same, Snap,* he said to himself. He continued to walk and searched until he found the one seagull he thought was following him. The bird would fly over him and find a place to perch just long enough for Snap to notice him and then fly away. This went on several times until finally the seagull swooped down in front of him and rested on the sand. That's when Snap noticed something in its mouth.

"My necklace! You have my necklace!"

The seagull squawked and dodged Snap's hand as he leapt for it.

"Give it back!" Snap took off after the gull. As he chased him, the gull flew low to the ground, never letting Snap reach him and never flying completely away either.

"What is this, some kind of game? Give me back my necklace!"

Turtle Town: The Inner Puka

The chase continued for a moment before Snap realized the bird was leading him somewhere. He stopped trying to reach for the necklace and instead followed the bird until it led him down to a cave entrance on the other side of the cove.

Snap followed cautiously, uncertain what might be waiting for him, and when they finally reached the inside of the cave, the seagull dropped the necklace and flew away. *Dude, what's going on?* He walked a few steps into the cave, then paused, thinking perhaps it was some sort of trap. The first animal who came to his mind was Lucas.

The inside of the cave was dark, and it echoed the sounds of the waves that crashed along the shoreline outside. It was damp and looked very scary. He reached down to pick up the necklace. He blew the sand off it and held it close to him, as though he were holding his mother's hand. "Thank goodness," he said under his breath. Snap looked around the unfamiliar place. The cave seemed to go on forever. He backed up slowly, holding tightly to the necklace in his hand. He felt along the ground with his feet, one step at a time, until suddenly he heard a voice echo from deep within the cave.

"I know why you love that necklace so much."

The sound of the words seemed to move up his shell and cover him like the darkness of the cave. He quivered and shuffled backward. He clung tightly to the puka shells and fell over on his back. Snap struggled to roll over, knowing there was no one there to help him get off his back. He froze when the voice spoke again.

"No need to be scared, Snap Shell."

Snap didn't know what else to do but remain still and respond. "How do you know my name?"

"I know everything about you, Snap."

"Everything?"

Snap Faces His Inner Cave

"Yes. I know why you cling to that necklace and hold it so tightly."

"How?" Snap stared into the dark cave, trying to focus on where the voice was coming from.

"The same way I knew you would come here today. The ocean is the life force of all turtles, and each of us is bound by the great inner puka. And that same life force that creates all turtle life in the world also binds us together, shows us our true destiny and challenges us to become our true self."

"Us?" Snap asked.

"Yes, us. The great species of the turtle."

"So, you're a turtle?"

The cave became quiet, and suddenly a huge green sea turtle came out of the darkness. Snap's eyes grew large as he made out the image before him. The sea turtle had the most beautiful shell he had ever seen. The turtle's face was firm, yet friendly, soft, yet rugged, youthful, but aged. Snap said the first thing that came to his mind. "Wrinklebutt?"

The turtle smiled. "I prefer Shelly, but what can I say, the rumors and folklore precede me." Wrinklebutt moved in closer and said, "I see your mother gave my necklace to you."

"What?" *My mother?* You mean this really *was* your necklace?" Snap stared at the collection of shells in his hand and tried to determine how his mother would have come to possess such a significant item. "But how? I mean, *how* did you know my mom?"

Wrinklebutt moved in closer and just smiled.

Snap couldn't help but go on. "The dreams? I saw you. I saw all three of us. Together. My mom was there, and *you* were there. How could this be?"

"Because we are connected, Snap Shell."

"By this?" Snap held up the necklace.

"Yes. You have the spirit of your mom, Snap. She was a very talented surfer, too."

Snap was completely shocked. "My mom surfed?"

"Yes, I used to be her teacher. Her mentor. I met her here many years ago, before she met your father."

"My father?" *What in the world?*

"Yes, your father, Snap. Your mother met your father here, many years ago."

Snap thought about the history of his family and all the little things he picked up on in conversation. *That's it,* he thought. "My mom and dad used to live in California," he said in amazement.

Wrinklebutt smiled and said, "And you, too."

"I did?"

"I'm your godmother, dear boy."

"You are?"

Wrinklebutt asked Snap to walk with her toward the cave entrance and the sea. "You see, you lived here the first year of your life."

"Then why did we ever leave? And why does my father despise the ocean so much if it's a part of our lives?"

Wrinklebutt's face became saddened. Snap waited for her to answer. "Your parents have traveled for your father's job for as long as I've known them. His business moved to the south." She looked at the ground and sighed.

Snap could tell something was just not right. "That's not it. There's more huh?"

"You truly are wiser than your years, my son."

Snap felt a chill run down his shell when she called him her son.

Wrinklebutt put her flipper to Snap's chin and looked into his eyes. "What's bothering you, dear?"

Snap Faces His Inner Cave

Snap didn't know where to begin. He felt like he didn't know who he was anymore or what he wanted, or for that matter, where he belonged.

"You can tell me." The old turtle smiled.

"Well, Shelly? Would you rather me call you Shelly?"

"Yes, that would be nice." Wrinklebutt winked.

"It's just." He paused, "How did my mom do it, Shelly?"

"You mean surf with the sea turtles?"

"Well yeah." Snap's eyes widened.

"She stayed true to herself, my dear. Her true self."

Well that sounds a lot easier than it seems, he thought. "Do you know how many sea turtles are talking about me? Telling rumors. Saying I can only surf because of this dumb necklace? Everyone here thinks it's the only reason why I'm any good. They think it's magic. It *is* magic, isn't it?"

"No, my dear. It is not magic. The magic is inside of you."

"I don't know. I couldn't even get up on my board today when I didn't have the necklace on. Maybe I just don't belong here." He paused and let out a deep puff of air through his nose holes. "But, I just don't know where I would go."

Wrinklebutt listened and said, "Do you know what the *Oia'i'o* symbol stands for?" Wrinklebutt took the necklace from Snap's hand and tapped it with a flipper.

"Yeah, isn't it Hawaiian or something?"

The old turtle nodded. "What do *you* want for yourself, Snap Shell?" Wrinklebutt asked while putting the necklace back around Snap's neck. "You wear this necklace for a reason, Snap. You must figure out what that reason is."

Snap didn't have an answer. "All I know is that I don't fit in here." Snap turned around and realized it was starting to get dark, and he had a long way back home.

"That's because you're a leader Snap, not a follower. Life isn't about fitting in."

Snap thought about it for a moment. He actually agreed. He had always been different.

"I know, you must go," Wrinklebutt smiled.

"Yeah, I'm already on my dad's bad side. I'm sure he isn't going to be happy that I'm getting home after dark again." Snap looked back up at Wrinklebutt, "Will I ever see you again? I mean, no one knows you're here, right?"

"You'll know where to find me."

"Do you live here?"

Wrinklebutt started walking back into the cave without answering.

I don't understand. Snap stood there, holding his necklace against his shell. He now had more questions than before he entered the cave. The more he thought about the situation the more he realized that maybe his questions weren't meant for Wrinklebutt. "It's Pops, isn't it?"

Wrinklebutt's words echoed in the dark as her silhouette disappeared into the cave. "Find you inner puka, Snap."

Once Snap made it back to Cardiff Beach, he walked through the front door of his house and into the kitchen to find *The Daily Shell* Newspaper spread open to page five on the table. Snap's article about the predicted winners for Surf Barrel 39 was big and bold.

"When were you going to tell me?"

Snap Faces His Inner Cave

A wave of panic rushed through him, and he turned around to find his dad. "You lied to me yesterday. You were already in the competition," Mr. Shell said in a deep and low voice.

"It's not even true, Pops. It's all made up. They do that in these papers. It was the hermit crab. He made it up," Snap said in desperation.

"I told you not to trust that crab! So you're telling me you didn't lie?" his father asked.

"Yes!" Snap yelled, but suddenly he became flooded with a wave of anger. "Yeah, Pops, I didn't lie. I'm not the one who lied at all."

"What's that supposed to mean, son?"

"It means I'm not the one who hasn't told the truth."

Mr. Shell moved in closer to his son. "What are you talking about?"

"I'm talking about mom!"

Mr. Shell was confused. "Your mother? What does your mother have to do with you not being honest with *me*?"

"She used to surf, didn't she Pops? She used to surf the same beaches I'm surfing today, didn't she? And I wonder how many times my toes touched the waters here in California when I was a baby, before I arrived with you this summer."

Mr. Shell was frozen. He said nothing.

"And Wrinklebutt? My godmother? What about her Pops? She used to teach mom, didn't she?"

"How?" Mr. Shell could barely speak. He began fumbling for words.

"I was born in California. What else did you and mom not tell me?"

Mr. Shell plopped himself into a chair. Snap couldn't move from the spot where he was standing.

"So, Shelly's back?"

Turtle Town: The Inner Puka

"What's going on Pops? How come there is so much I learned today that *you* haven't told me?" Snap wanted answers so badly.

"I guess you're old enough to know everything." Mr. Shell sighed. Snap waited.

"Yes, son, your mother did surf. She was just like you. She wore flippers, she didn't care what the sea turtles thought, and she walked on two feet." Mr. Shell paused and said quietly, "Just not around me."

Snap stood there, not saying a word, waiting again for his dad to continue.

"She was the only box turtle who dared to be different. Not only that, but she and Shelly were two of the only female surfers here in Turtle Town back then. Shelly was much older than your mom, and when Shelly found out your mom wanted to compete, she trained her."

Snap's eyes and ears were open and taking in every word as he waited to hear more.

"Your mom competed for a few years and got really good. She was never as good as Shelly, but she kept up. Shelly, or *Wrinklebutt,* as most call her, because of her damaged back shell, well, she's a legend. She even trained Timmy years ago when he was very young."

"So you and mom knew Timmy, too?" Snap asked. It all started to make sense. Timmy knew everything.

"Well, Timmy was known as Little Tim back then," his father started again. "He was only a teenager when your mom used to surf." Mr. Shell paused for what seemed like forever before he continued. "A few days after your egg hatched and you were born, your mom surfed in Surf Barrel 29."

Snap listened as Mr. Shell's voice got a little shaky. He rubbed his eyes and continued. "There was an accident, Snap. Your mom wiped out and her head hit the rocks under the ocean. I couldn't do anything, and Wrinklebutt swam out to save her. She was under for a really long time. It was the scariest moment of my life. I was completely helpless, and honestly, I was too scared to even attempt to save her. I mean, I was *completely* helpless. I couldn't swim. I could only hope, pray, and watch the lifeguards and Wrinklebutt as they carried her body to the shore."

Snap's eyes started to water as his dad continued the story.

"After they resuscitated her, I promised myself I would always protect her. I would never let anything happen to her."

"That's when we moved, isn't it?" Snap questioned.

"Yes. Your mother and I agreed on Houston, Texas as our new home, since it wasn't far from the gulf where I worked."

"But what about the time when we moved to Galveston Beach?" Snap questioned.

"I thought we both could handle it by then. It had been seven years since her accident. I really needed to be in Galveston for my job, and I hated being away from you and your mom. I saw that being by the water and not surfing was still hard for her to handle because she missed it so much."

"I remember. She used to take me to the beach every day in the summer."

"I know, son. Unfortunately, after the hurricane, we had no choice but to move back to Houston where it was safe."

Snap walked over to the kitchen table to sit down.

Out of nowhere, Mr. Shell broke down. "Your mother's death was devastating. I didn't protect her. I wasn't there. I couldn't stop that car. I broke my promise." Mr. Shell had never said those words before, not even in previous counseling sessions he attended privately. He held his hands to his face and began to cry.

Snap moved toward his father and put one hand on his father's shell. He hated to see his dad upset. "But Pops, it wasn't your fault. You have to let it all go. We all must live our own lives, right?"

"I know son, you are right. I can't do the same to you. I can't hold you back from living your life." Mr. Shell put his hand in his son's.

"What are you saying then?" Snap looked into his dad's eyes.

"I'm saying if you want to compete, if you want to surf, I will be there. I will be at your competition. I will cheer on my only son and support you the way your mother would expect me to. The way she would, if she were still here."

Snap didn't know what to say. He couldn't believe that all of this was happening at once.

"Really?"

"Yes, really. I am so proud of you. You are the pride and joy of my life, Snap. Every time I see you, I see your mother's spirit living in you. And every time you dare to be different or challenge life by living it to the fullest, it reminds me of her and all the amazing things she brought into my life. Into our life."

Snap hugged his dad. He realized just how badly he wanted to compete at that very moment. "Thank you, Pops. I won't let you down. I promise." Snap kissed his dad and held him for a moment longer before running to his room. The first animal he wanted to tell was Iggy. He wanted to share his great news with his best friend in the whole world, his true friend, and tell him all the history he learned about himself today. Snap picked up the phone and dialed Iggy's number. When Iggy's little sister Molly picked up the phone, Snap was even excited to hear her voice.

"Hey, Molly! It's Snap. What are you doing?"

"Well, Snap, I'm glad you asked, being that you called at such a late hour. You know we are in Central Standard Time here, right!? But, since you asked, I am painting my nails!" She started to share all the details about the color she was using when Snap cut her off.

"Sorry, Molly. I just have some great news to tell Iggy. Can I talk to him?"

"Well, if you insist. He is probably checking on the egg."

"Oh, yeah. I forgot. You're going to be a big sister."

"Don't remind me. That egg has taken up all of my time and energy already."

Snap started to laugh at the fact that five-year old little Molly had no responsibilities and loved to over-exaggerate her stories.

"Let me go find him," she said.

Two seconds later, Iggy was on the phone. "Snap! You called! Is everything okay? I mean, it's kinda late, but I'm sure glad you called me!" In his excitement, Iggy spoke quickly.

"Yeah, yeah man. Everything is great! I just wanted to update you on the good news." Snap told Iggy all about the competition, his meeting with Wrinklebutt, the truth about his life, his mom, and even about the drama on the beach. It felt so good to get everything off his shell. By the time they hung up the phone, it was past midnight.

Chapter 10

The Shack

Wrinklebutt was grilling seaweed when Snap walked into the cave the next day. He couldn't wait to tell her that he knew everything and was ready to find out what *he* wanted.

"I knew you would be back," she smiled.

Snap sat down while she offered him a grilled weed. He felt like it would be rude if he didn't take it, even though he wasn't fond of the food.

Snap wasted no time and told Wrinklebutt all about his talk with his father. Even though many of his questions had been answered, he still had one on his mind. "So why did you leave California a few years ago? I mean, my friends, well they used to be my friends until this whole competition and necklace gossip started, they said you were the best surfer here. You're a legend. That's what my dad called you too."

Wrinklebutt smiled at Snap's compliments. "I left and swam to the gulf when I learned your mother died. She was like a daughter to me." Wrinklebutt paused to gather her thoughts, "I knew you had the necklace and something in the great puka of life told me you would find your way back to the ocean. So, I came back to find you."

Snap smiled. "For me?"

"You are very special, Snap."

"Sometimes I feel like I'm not special, that maybe the only thing special about me is this necklace."

"I could feel that you were having difficulties being here, especially with your father. It was time for you to know your history. But you know, your dad, he still carries fear. He wasn't always that way, but as animals grow older and we become comfortable and bound to the animals who make up our lives, well, we become so attached that we can't imagine a life without them. You are your father's strength, my dear child. You are everything to him now, and even though he loves the ocean, he will always fear what she is capable of taking from him. You, like your mother and myself, never let our fear or differences stop us from being our best. From being great. It's one of the many things we have in common."

"So does that mean my gift is the fact that I'm different?"

"That is the greatest gift in each of us, Snap. That is why you wear the *Oia'i'o* symbol. It stands for the true self. The inner puka in each of us that binds us together, to the sea, to all life. You are not like the other turtles here, Snap."

"I know." Snap held up his blue flipper.

"Not just on the outside. It is unfortunate the way the community has started to change around here, because we are all turtles, and we shouldn't discriminate against each other."

"That's what I said."

"And that is why I haven't come back until now. It will take a turtle like you, young, vibrant, and respected to change things on the beach. An event will happen when you return. An event that

The Shack

will affect everything for you and your friends. Only you have the power to change it."

Snap started to get worried. "What? An event? Not another earthquake?" Snap wondered in the back of his mind, what she meant by when *he returned*.

"It will feel bad."

Dude, that's not reassuring. "Me? I'm just one turtle? What can I do? Besides that, everyone is suspicious of me."

"Turtles, or all species for that matter, are suspicious of anything we don't fully understand. Ask yourself, why do you want to compete in Surf Barrel 39? Is it to beat Lucas? Is it to impress Tula? Do you feel bad for all of the time Timmy has spent training you and not others? Are you afraid of losing? What do you want? What are your biggest fears at the end of the day? Those are the questions you have to answer, for they are the obstacles you have to overcome."

Snap stood there, speechless. He couldn't believe Wrinklebutt said all of that. It was like she was reading his mind or had somehow been watching him since the first day he walked into surf school.

"You'll know what to do in the end. I have faith in you, but now, you must come with me."

"Are we going far? I don't want to worry my father if I am gone too long. He's kind of a worry wart, you know."

"My gull will send him a note. When he sees it's from me, I promise, he will understand." Wrinklebutt picked up a feather from off the ground. "Now, where did I leave my stationary pad and ink?" She looked behind a few rocks, eventually pulling out her writing utensils to scribble a quick note. Wrinklebutt waved to the big sea gull who had taken Snap's necklace, handed him the note, and the bird flew off without hesitation.

"Is this kind of like in those movies when the teacher takes the student away to a faraway place to learn karate or something?"

"Well, I do have a black belt, but no, you will not be doing karate where we're going." Wrinklebutt walked toward the water and signaled for Snap to follow her. Snap could feel his stomach tighten in anticipation; he was nervous, but he trusted Wrinklebutt's decisions.

He slid down a rock into the water and held his breath. He could tell the water was getting warmer now that the marine layer had finally left for the summer. He opened his eyes under water and focused on the back of Wrinklebutt's shell. It was completely deformed and closed up at the end, giving her tail a crooked look. *Dude, now I get it,* he thought. The name *Wrinklebutt* made more sense when he saw it.

The turtles swam south together, and every few minutes, Wrinklebutt came up for air to allow a breathing break for Snap. Holding his breath underwater got easier as the swim went on. At the last break, Wrinklebutt guided Snap toward the shore.

"Welcome to Silver Strand," she said with a wink. "Over there, you will see the Coronado Bridge."

"Wow!" Snap pulled out his map to locate their destination point. "Cool. There it is on the map."

"You're still using that old map, dear child?" Wrinklebutt questioned. "Where did you find this thing? It looks like part of the Dead Sea Scrolls."

"Um, Trek gave it to me. I'm just using it until I know this place like the back of my shell." In his own defense, he said, "I'm a visual learner, that's all."

"You are your mother's child." Wrinklebutt's gaze turned into a humbled smile. "Very well." Wrinklebutt set one flipper on Snap's head, almost as if doing some kind of blessing.

The Shack

"What are we doing out here?"

"Well, I suppose we will do a little surfing, but first, we must stop by my home."

"But I thought you left California?"

"I did. But I still have a place here when I do visit." Wrinklebutt pointed toward a huge building that looked almost like an old abandoned castle. "The hotel attendants are sworn to secrecy," she said. "No one says a word when I return. That's the deal." She started to move forward then added, "Oh, they store my boards too." Wrinklebutt paused and looked around, as if making sure none of the vacationers noticed her. Snap figured that was normal, after all, she was a legend.

The more and more Snap looked at the old turtle's shell, the more interested he became in her life story. The marks on each section really did look like the cave carvings he imagined in his dream. Her shell was so beautiful. He couldn't stop staring. The aquatic colors blended from one to the other almost as if her shell were changing colors in the sunlight.

"Come. Follow me."

Snap followed Wrinklebutt to what looked to be a barn or a shack at the side of the castle-like building. Wrinklebutt unlocked three separate deadbolts to gain entrance. When the door swung open, Wrinklebutt flicked on a light switch, and twenty different colored spotlights came on, one after the other. Snap was amazed to see what was inside the room. *Surfboards!* There were rows and rows of surfboards in every color of the rainbow. There were various shapes for every type of body size and turtle shell imaginable. They were the best brands in the history of surfing. Some were aged and made out of balsa wood. If Snap wasn't mistaken, there was even a board with the year 1985 engraved in diamond shells.

"Well, here's my board collection. I have been collecting these for over forty years. I won about half of them."

Snap gulped and remained speechless.

"Come inside," she said.

Snap slowly walked into the shack, and Wrinklebutt closed the door behind them.

"No one knows this place exists, huh?" Snap said while feeling over the diamond engraved board. "Pipeline Masters?" he gasped.

"Yes, that was my 10th year to place." Wrinklebutt confirmed.

"So, is this where you live too?"

"I don't need much."

Snap looked around and noticed a cot on the floor.

"I'm sure you thought I lived in the big castle, right?" Wrinklebutt asked when she noticed Snap looking around the room.

Snap nodded.

"Riches and images of what other turtles think about us is not everything in this world. Only one thing truly matters. Love."

"Well, that's simple enough," Snap said.

"But it's not. It's more of an appreciation, an acceptance. It's an appreciation for the beginning, not just the end, but truly finding yourself in the moment and being one with the ocean of life. That's what love is all about to the soul surfer."

"That's deep." Snap nodded, then asked, "Is that why you do it?"

"Do what, compete? Or surf?"

"I don't know. Both I guess?"

"I compete because I like the challenge, and I like setting a goal. I compete to push myself, not for the prizes." She leaned in toward Snap and added, "But they are nice."

Snap nodded his head, feeling as though he could somehow relate.

"I surf for one reason and one reason only. To become one with a force in nature that is bigger than anything in this world."

"You mean the ocean?" Snap asked.

"That's right, my dear. The ocean. The only place turtles can completely lose themselves *and* find themselves at the same exact moment is in the sea. That means *all* turtles, in my opinion. Surfing allows all of us a chance to experience the true source of our might."

"Lose ourselves?" Snap thought he understood what she was saying, but wanted to learn more.

"You see, surfing has the capability to completely take over your thought process until it becomes you. Soul surfing. It becomes a part of who you are as you find yourself out in the ocean. The ocean is the most sacred place for turtles, Snap."

"Even box shells?"

"Yes. Even box shells who wear blue flippers." She smiled.

"Hmmm. So it's kind of like those animals who can play the piano without even thinking about what they're doing. They just play?"

"Just like that. They become the music. It's an art. Surfing is an art. And I know how much you love your art, Snap. I want you to understand surfing like I do, like your mother did, before you compete in this competition." Wrinklebutt looked him directly in the eyes and said, "It's not just about beating your opponent. It's more than that. Surfing in this competition is about competing with yourself, pushing yourself beyond your own limits and surpassing your innermost fears."

Snap started to imagine Lucas with his leather cuffs and his evil smile when she said the word, opponent. "Become one with the ocean," he paused, "and beat Lucas," he said under his breath.

"Defeat your fears," Wrinklebutt corrected him. Wrinklebutt handed Snap an anniversary edition

Tortuga surfboard. "Take this, we will surf at sunset together."

"No way. You're going to let me use this?" Snap hesitated. "In the water?"

"It's yours, godson. No need to borrow any more boards from anyone else. You need to have one of your own."

"Wow! Thank you." Snap held the board with both hands, focusing on the shadowy reflection in the enamel colored fiberglass.

"We got that one in Hawaii. My second home away from home."

"Dude," Snap said. "Hawaii?"

"It's a whole different world there."

"I would like to go one day."

"And you will." Wrinklebutt grabbed a longboard of her own, decorated in heavily detailed lines of red and black. Motioning for the door, she asked, "Ready? The sun does not wait on those who are late."

Snap eagerly picked up his new board and followed Wrinklebutt out the door. "Look!" Snap pointed toward the sun. "There isn't much time." It had grown much dimmer outside, and Snap could see the sun sitting in the middle of the sky, just above the water's edge.

"This is my favorite part of the day. Nothing compares to surfing at sunset," she said.

Snap didn't realize there was so much philosophy to surfing, and Wrinklebutt's comparison to life was way beyond anything he could imagine. He was starting to love the way she talked to him, in code sometimes. The two turtles walked toward the triangular reflection of the sun on the water with their boards under their arms.

Once their feet hit the dampened sand, Snap froze.

"What's the matter?"

Snap looked down at his necklace.

"You are the same with or without it, Snap. Everything you need to succeed is already inside you."

"So, any advice, then?"

"Get in the water, and find your strength," she said. "I've given you all the advice you need. Get in the water, Snap Shell, the box shell turtle from Texas." She motioned for him to leave her behind.

"Snap Shell the box shell turtle from *California*," he said under his breath. He shuffled into the water and dropped his belly to his board. Wrinklebutt was right about surfing at sunset. It was a completely mesmerizing experience.

As he paddled out toward the fading sun and the darkening ocean, he couldn't help but notice a scratched engraving in the surfboard. It was the *'Oia'i'o* symbol. Snap thought about what the symbol really meant to him. It was easy to worry about everyone watching him, judging him, but out here, that didn't matter. In the ocean, all that mattered was how much he enjoyed the privilege of experiencing life.

"Shelly?" Snap threw his head over his shoulder to see if she was coming out. He wanted to share with her his thoughts on the symbol, but she was gone. He could feel she was watching him even though at that moment, he was all alone. If he was going to compete, no one else was going to do it for him. *It's time,* he thought to himself. He wanted it and he felt he was ready.

The box turtle knew what he had to do. He paddled his surfboard beyond the point break and turned to face the shore. He was going to ride *with* the ocean this time, even if it took him under. There was no turning back.

Chapter 11
Soul Surfing

Snap Shell stayed the remainder of the week with Wrinklebutt, learning about life from the old soul who had traveled all over the ocean. He ate from the orange trees and berry bushes, learned what it was like to live with the bare essentials and he finally grew an appetite for seaweed and kelp. Wrinklebutt never showed off her talent while teaching Snap how to surf from the soul. She didn't have to. Snap respected her words of wisdom.

The last evening before Wrinklebutt told Snap it was time to go home, Snap spent some time out on the waves by himself. His transformation was apparent. Snap had received the gifts from his teacher and applied them into every aspect of his life, surfing the waves with the wind and break as in sync as a flock of migrating black birds.

When Snap came back to the shack after his last surf at Silver Strand, Wrinklebutt was nowhere to be found. She had set his map on the pallet she made for him each night. *She must not be very good at goodbyes,* he thought to himself. He hoped it wasn't the last time he would see her, and he fought back a few tears before making the move back to Cardiff.

Once he got home, he wasn't in the mood to explain why he skipped surf school for a week or tell anyone where and why he had disappeared, so he went straight to his house to see his dad. Mr. Shell was reading the paper when Snap walked in the door.

"Hi son, how was your journey?"

"Hey, Pops." Snap stood there for a moment in awkward silence. "You know where I was, right?"

Mr. Shell nodded his head and smiled. Snap fell over in his beanbag chair and sighed. "Shelly said you would understand."

"It is okay, son." Mr. Shell folded up his newspaper and reclined back in his fuzzy brown chair. "I have to admit though, it was pretty lonely here with you gone all week. Your friends have been asking about you too. I ran into them at the Turtle Society meeting. They were having a big beach clean-up."

"Really?" *I'm surprised,* he thought. "So I guess that means they haven't forgotten about me?" Snap couldn't help but make the comment.

"I hope you learned what you needed from Shelly. She's possibly the wisest turtle you will ever meet, son," his father said. His father adjusted his shell and said, "Well, *almost* the wisest. I'm proud that she is your godmother." Mr. Shell paused for a moment and said, "I hope you don't have ill feelings toward me, son. You know, for not telling you all of this before now. The last turtle I want to let down in this entire world is you, Snap."

"It's okay, Pops." Snap picked himself off the beanbag to hug his dad goodnight. "I'm going to get ready for bed. I'm pretty tired." He turned to go upstairs and heard his father say quietly, "I'm proud of you."

Soul Surfing

After Snap brushed his teeth, he walked over to his laptop to check the weather and surf report for tomorrow. The first thing he noticed was a message from his best friend, sent earlier that morning.

Dear Snap,
I can't believe Wrinklebutt was real! And your godmother? You will never believe the dream I had last night! I was driving down the coast with my family in a convertible, and we were passing all these billboards, you know ads for sunscreen, surf camps, sailboats... We were coming to visit you in Cardiff Beach. We passed all these turtles and walruses and seals on the road. Molly even thought she saw Olive on rollerblades. You remember Molly's best friend, Olive, right? The little Red Ear Slider. Well, they all had surfboards... it was so cool! But then we passed by this one billboard and YOU were on it! You had won a surf competition and you were like the first surfing box shell turtle in the world or something. You had your flippers on and everything! What if it was a sign?
    Iggy

Snap couldn't wait to fill Iggy in on everything he learned from his godmother. After emailing him back, the tired box shell fell asleep on the keyboard to his laptop computer. Snap was so exhausted that he slept at his desk until the sun, peering through his window, woke him up the next morning.

Walking into surf school the next day was one of the most awkward moments in Snap's very young life. Every single student fell silent and studied him as he walked to his usual spot in the sand, even Timmy. How was Snap supposed to explain where he had been for a week? He knew that his godmother wouldn't want him to tell about her secret hiding place, much less give away her identity.

Lucas was the first to make a comment. "So, look who's back. I figured you ran back or should I say, waddled back home to Texas on all fours." The class started to laugh and then were stopped short by Timmy.

"That's enough, Lucas. It's none of anyone's business where Snap's been." Timmy motioned for everyone to turn around and pay attention to him so he could begin class.

"Wait! Your necklace!" Tula was the first to notice. "You got your necklace back. But how?"

Snap nodded and put one finger up to his mouth signaling for Tula not to say anything. He didn't want to draw any more attention to his *disappearance*. He whispered to her and said, "I'll explain later." *I think.*

As class began, the students followed Timmy outside, where he separated the turtles into pairs. One turtle stayed on the shore, while the other went out into the water. Each turtle's partner had to critique the other's rail riding technique. Snap was partnered with Tula. *This will be interesting*, Snap thought. The last time Snap saw Tula she was still ignoring him. Today, though, she seemed to be over what was bugging her and more curious about him than anything.

"Okay, this is just weird. First you're gone for a week, then you get your necklace back, and *this*?" Tula grabbed Snap's new *Tortuga* board. "A *Tortuga* thruster? Seriously, where have you been, dude?"

Snap figured some of the turtles would notice his new board, especially Timmy. He hadn't come up with a believable story to tell, yet. "Come on Tula, I'll tell you later. It's a long story."

"Fine." She shook her bill at him and headed for the water. To everyone's surprise, Tula and Snap outdid most of the others in the morning class. Judging by Timmy's comments, it had become apparent to Snap that Timmy recognized his level of skill definitely had improved. Snap's rides were so smooth and steady. He also noticed that Tula's rides were exceptionally strong, and it looked like she had been practicing too. The more they worked together in pairs, the more Snap felt confident and secure in his decision to enter the Surf Barrel 39 Competition.

When class ended that day, Timmy said that he had something important to talk to everyone about. The class sat down and waited to hear what he had to say. "So, surfer dudes," Timmy paused to clear his throat. "For those of you who actually read the paper, you may have seen the article this morning about the Trestles Beach shut down."

Everyone, including Snap, looked around at each other in shock. Obviously, no one had read the story.

"It has been in the works for a while now, but the county has decided to build a road through Trestles Beach."

"What? When? How?" The whole class started asking questions. Snap and Lucas looked at each other.

"As many of you know, Trestles Beach is where the surf competition has been held for many years. The surf there is excellent and like no other here in Southern California."

Snap's heart started to beat at a rapid pace.

"I'm sure all of you can understand what this means," Timmy continued.

"No Surf Barrel?" Slide yelled.

"I'm sorry, but there is nothing I can do about this. I've talked to as many animals as I could, and unfortunately, this is out of my flippers. I'm sorry." Timmy turned around with his head held low and walked back to the surf shop with Herbert and Star following behind.

"Such a pity," Herbert said with Star nodding in agreement.

"No way! There has to be a way to stop it!" Snap spoke up.

"Like what?" Lucas asked. "You think there is anything *you* can do about it?"

Snap didn't respond. He ignored the fact that Lucas was right and secondly, he was shocked the Leatherback hadn't charged at him as soon as Timmy turned his back.

"Do you think your pops would know what to do?" Tula whispered to Snap.

"My dad only does microorganism research, Tula. He doesn't save the beaches, just researches them."

Snap walked away feeling awful. Everything he just went through would have been for nothing if he couldn't compete in this competition.

"Wait!" Snap had a thought and stopped to turn back around when he remembered what Wrinklebutt had told him. She said that something horrible would happen, something that only he would be able to fix. *Is this what she meant?*

Tula waited for him to respond, hoping perhaps her friend had come up with an idea and a way to save the beach and the competition. "Maybe you're right, Tula. Maybe my dad *can* help," Snap said.

"How?" Tula asked.

"I don't know, but I'm pretty sure this is one of those moments where I can either stand up and make a difference or sit back and do nothing."

Tula was so excited, she punched Snap in the arm, nearly knocking him over on his shell. "Really? How?" The commotion raised everyone's attention, and a few other turtles gathered around to listen.

Snap thought for a moment then started to give orders. "Spike. Go get Herb and Trek. Tula, you said you were part of the turtle society, right?"

"Yeah."

"Well, I have an idea, and I'm going to need your help."

Lucas came up to Snap with his usual attitude. "*What in the beach* do you think you can do, box brain?"

"Listen, Lucas. Do you want to beat me in the competition or not?"

"More than anything, B.T. I would like to *wipe…you…out*," he said, poking Snap in the chest to accentuate his words.

"Okay, then. Just trust me. You will have your competition, and you'll get your chance. I just need you to cooperate. I need *all of us*, to work together for a change."

"Okay, B.T. On one condition," Lucas said.

"What?"

"You surf without your silly little necklace." Lucas smirked and put his flipper around Tula's shoulder.

Snap heard the subtle whisper of Wrinklebutt's words replaying in his mind—*everything you need to succeed is already inside you*. Without hesitation, Snap agreed. "Fine. It's a deal. No necklace." The two turtles shook on it, as the crowd witnessed.

"So, what brainy idea do you have in mind, anyway?" Lucas asked and grabbed Snap's board from his hands. Lucas inspected the writing across the nose and looked Snap dead in the eyes. "Where did you get this?"

"None of your business, jellyfish breath." Snap grabbed his board from Lucas' strong grip and kept on, ignoring any type of intimidation the Leatherback was trying to throw his way.

Harry and a few of the other Hawksbills laughed under their breath, impressed by Snap's gutsy response.

Herbert, Star, Trekker and Spike came back in to join the group of turtles on the beach. For the first time ever, the little box shell turtle was able to get Hawksbills, Olive Ridleys, and even Leatherbacks to join together in one group, for one mission.

"Herbert!" Snap said.

"*Monsieur*!" he responded.

"I need you to meet me at Starlucks Coffee Shop tomorrow morning, bright and early, ready to write an article for *The Daily Shell*."

"You can count on me, *monsieur*. Coffee and biscuits will be on Star." The sea star shook his head *no*.

"Great," Snap said. "Now, Tula. I need you to meet me at my house tonight. We are going to start doing research with my dad for Herbert's article." Tula nodded her head and punched Lucas before he had an opportunity to throw out a wise crack.

"Harry. I need you and all the Hawksbills to start making 'Save Trestles' signs."

"Got it, brah."

"Spike. I need you, Barney, Mossy, and Slide to go down to Trestles tomorrow. Take pictures and notes about all the different surf breaks. Count how many animals surf there in one day. Got it?"

"Got it!" Spike nudged Snap and added, "You're a pretty cool box shell, dude."

Snap grinned in response, then turned and said, "Lucas?"

"What?"

"I need you and your bale to work with your gulls and all the Hawksbills to get those flyers put up all over town."

Before Lucas would agree, he asked Snap, "And what are you going to do?"

"I'm organizing this whole operation, *and*," he paused and puffed out his shell, "I'm going to give the speech at the press conference that will be set up by Timmy and Trek for us this Saturday. I need everyone to be there!" Snap looked over at Trekker.

"What do you know about press?" Lucas asked, rolling his eyes.

"I bet with Trek and Timmy's help, we can get a press conference set in no time. I mean, they do it on TV all the time!"

"Whatever. Fine. We'll see if you can pull this off," Lucas said.

Trekker let out an energetic *Phfff* and ran back to the shop as if he had already come up with a plan to get the media and press on board. "I'm on it!" *Phfff.*

"Alright! Everyone knows what they need to do! Tula, I'll see you at my house in an hour." Everyone scattered, and Snap hurried off to talk to his dad. When he got home, he burst through the door to find his dad in the kitchen. "Pops! We need to know how to save a beach!" Snap said with purpose.

His father was excited to hear his son so interested in doing conservationist work. "Well, I am a member of the CCG," his father chuckled.

"Huh?"

"The California Conservation Group," Mr. Shell confirmed.

"Perfect!" Snap didn't know what that meant, but it sounded important.

"What's going on, son?" Mr. Shell questioned.

"What do you know about Trestles, Pops?"

"Oh. You're talking about that toll road they want to put through the beach park."

"Well, yeah. You know that is where the surfing competition is? Or, is *supposed to be* this year."

Mr. Shell bit his lip. "Oh, honestly son, I guess I didn't even put two and two together. That's not good. Have they already started to shut everything down?"

"They will next week. That's the week of Surf Barrel!"

Mr. Shell couldn't think of anything to say.

"So I need your help, Pops, to stop them by this Saturday."

"Saturday? Uh, well son, how do you plan to do that?"

"Trek and Timmy are going to try to set up a press conference. I've got the whole surf school working on it."

"Wow, son. That's a pretty big job for y'all."

"Everyone's working together on this, even Lucas."

"Who is Lucas?" his father asked.

Snap stopped moving around long enough to look his father straight in the eyes. "Let's just say, he's the turtle I'm going to beat at the surf competition this year."

"Okay, so how do you want me to help?"

"So, you're in?"

"I don't think I have much of a choice, do I?"

"Great! Tula is coming over too. We want you to teach us everything you know about conserving the wildlife and environment of Trestles. Herbert is going to write an article for *The Daily Shell*."

"Well, do you have time to eat dinner?" Mr. Shell sat a plate in front of Snap.

"You made dinner?"

"Your favorite. Veggie Burgers!"

"Sweet! Can Tula eat with us?"

Mr. Shell had barely agreed when the doorbell rang, and Tula let herself in. "I'm here!"

"Come in, Tula." Mr. Shell motioned for her to sit down.

After quickly inhaling their veggie burgers and sweet potato fries, Tula and Snap jumped on the Internet to begin researching the area.

Mr. Shell pulled out his environmental books to research the particular strains a road puts on the land conditions, animal life, climate, winds, and water force. The three took notes and discussed the topic for hours. By the end of the evening, Snap had pages of notes to take to Herbert in the morning.

"Well, kids. That's what I call good research. I'm going to finish up my own work if you two don't mind and head to bed." Mr. Shell patted his son on the shell and gave him a look that let his son know he was proud of him. "Good luck with your article." Mr. Shell hugged both turtles and left the kitchen.

Snap stood up to stretch, after sitting in his chair for so long. They needed a little break, so he had an idea. "Want to see the view from my top roof deck?" Snap knew Tula would love the view of the dark ocean and stars twinkling overhead. Snap hadn't been up there too many times but loved to look at the coastal view. She agreed, and he led her outside and up to the top of the house. The pair sat with their legs dangling through the rails of the top deck.

"I think you may have the highest view in all of Cardiff," Tula said, while gazing into the reflection of the full moon on the water. "You can see the entire coastal line. Look, you can even see Swami's surf break out in Encinitas!"

"Yeah, I love it up here," Snap said. He paused for a minute, thinking about how great it was to be around

Tula again and actually do something important for the beach with her. "We have to save Trestles, Tula. We just have to. When Timmy took me out to Lowers the other week, it was probably the best surf I've ever been in. It's different out there. I don't get why anyone would want to ruin such a perfect place."

"You've gotta say that if you get the chance then, Snap."

"I will. I know Trek and Timmy will do everything they can to help us, too."

Tula suddenly changed the subject. "So, I have a question." She didn't look at him, but instead kept her eyes focused straight ahead.

I knew this was coming, he thought. "Yeah?"

"Where were you?" she asked. "You just like, disappeared."

Snap remained silent and considered whether he could trust her with his story.

She continued on, "I know I was acting kind of weird toward you last week, but it was just a bad week, and well, Spike was putting all kinds of pressure on me for not hanging out *with my own kind.*" Tula sighed, never looking at Snap.

"Why does he think that's a big deal?"

"I don't know. It probably has something to do with Lucas," Tula told him.

Snap looked down at Tula's puka shell bracelet that she always wore. She was wearing two this time. He wanted to ask where the other one came from, assuming it was a gift, but she kept talking.

"I understand if you're still mad at me," she started. "But when you were gone, I missed you. And that's when I realized how great of a turtle you are, and a friend."

He hesitated before responding, and then realized she might be sincere. "Can you keep a secret?" Snap asked.

"Yeah, of course!" She smiled eagerly. "Totally!"

"No, I mean, like a real secret. The kind you can't tell anyone, not even Spike."

"Yes!" She squeaked.

"I don't know." Snap started to think it over, second guessing his decision.

Tula placed one flipper on his hand. "Snap, I'm sorry I was ever mean or turned my back on you. I know you're a real surfer."

Snap stood up and took a deep breath. "I met Wrinklebutt."

"What?!" Her eyes bulged. "When?" She grabbed his arm and pulled herself up, too.

"Last week."

"So, wait, is that why...?"

"Yep."

"All week?"

Snap laughed. "Yep."

"And the board?"

He nodded his head.

"Tell me everything!"

Snap filled Tula in on the entire story, leaving out only one small detail—the exact location to Wrinklebutt's California home. Tula understood why he couldn't tell her, and she was ecstatic to hear all about his journey, her surfboard collection, the story of his family history and the lessons he had with her. The pair sat together on the upper deck to his balcony and talked and talked about Wrinklebutt and their plans to save Trestles. When Tula finally went home, Snap watched her walk down the hill toward the huts and smiled the entire time.

Morning Coffee Buzz

Snap met Herbert and Star at Starlucks Coffee Shop bright and early to work on the article to save Trestles. To avoid another emotional outburst from Star, Snap graciously accepted the vanilla soy latte that Star bought for him. As the turtle slowly sipped his coffee while sitting among an entire coffee shop full of bouncing sea stars, he couldn't help but laugh and feel good about what he had gotten himself into. Starfish were typing away at unbelievable speeds on their miniature laptops. Other starfish lounged in chairs, debating over matters of concern, but in sign language. Snap and Herbert were the only ones talking, yet through the windows, it probably looked as if the entire shop was bouncing with loud chatter.

Snap looked up from his notes and spotted Trekker and Timmy as they walked through the door.

"Snap!" *Phfff.* "You two are already working hard, now that's snappy." *Phfff.*

Just then, Star slammed his coffee cup on the table, and Trekker added, "And you too Star." *Phfff.*

"Thanks. Herb is doing all the writing. We're almost done," Snap said.

"Precisely. I am an expert journalist," Herbert said. He put his head back down and tapped the tips of his claws on the keyboard to his own miniature laptop.

"We have good news," Timmy smiled. "The mayor is holding a hearing to address the communities' concerns about the road. The press will be there! *And*... we've got you on the agenda! It will be held on Saturday at 11:00 AM in Del Mar."

"Really!?" Snap was elated. "I'm speaking in front of the mayor?"

Herbert paused to clap his claws together, and Star slammed his cup on the table in approval.

Morning Coffee Buzz

"Well, it does help that one of the major reporters for Beach Break 8 News owes me a favor for supplying her whole family reunion of pelicans with Sea Trek Helmets." *Phfff.*

"Awesome!" Snap gave Trekker a high five.

"Then we'll add the hearing time to the article and publish it in tomorrow's paper," Snap said.

Herbert looked up toward the ceiling and said, "Oh, deadlines."

Timmy approved and said, "Perfect! That should get you some support. Keep up the good work, kids!"

Once the article was complete, Herbert handed his laptop over to Snap and Star for final approval.

"It looks great, Herb!" Snap said and realized this may be the first article of real importance that Herbert actually had the opportunity to write. Star, however, grabbed the laptop and shook his head *no*.

"What's wrong?" Snap looked down at the little star.

"Oh, don't pay attention to him. He just needs more coffee. Do you mind getting us another cup, Star?" Herbert said.

"Oh, please. No more for me." Snap could barely finish half of his caffeinated drink, and he kept getting the urge to run around the coffee shop. Star shook his head *yes*, got up from his seat, and headed straight for the restroom instead of the counter.

"Stubborn Star," Herbert chuckled. "Okay, let me know if you need anything else, *monsieur*."

"Thanks for your help, Herb," Snap said. "I totally appreciate it."

"No problem, *monsieur*. I would hate to see Surf Barrel go."

Snap got up and headed to the surf school to meet the rest of the team who had also been hard at work. The Hawksbills had made colorful signs and started roping them up to get ready to set up for the gulls to fly around the beaches. Spike had sent a gull to Snap to give him updates on the conditions at Trestles, but unfortunately, Snap didn't understand *Squawkery*. It took him ten minutes to convince Lucas to translate, with a little help from Tula.

"This is perfect information for my speech!" Snap tried to give Lucas a high five, but the arrogant Leatherback snorted and walked away.

They all continued to work together to prepare for the big day, then took a break for some late afternoon surfing, of course. Snap spent the last few hours of the day preparing the speech he was going to give on Saturday in Del Mar. They only had one more day to finalize everything. The article and signs would go out tomorrow.

On the morning of the Trestles hearing, Snap woke up with a knot in his stomach. Today was the day. The day he would prove that he could make a difference. It was a lot for one box shell to handle, and he was feeling the effects in his stomach.

"Green or blue?" he said to himself while going through his collection of ties hanging in his closet. Green seemed the most environmental friendly and inviting. He grabbed the forest green tie and walked in front of his bathroom mirror, replacing his necklace with the more appropriate accessory for the occasion. He needed to make a good impression. After waxing his shell, he came downstairs for breakfast.

"Are you feeling okay, son?" Mr. Shell handed Snap a bowl of fruit and granola.

"I'm nervous, Pops. I've never done anything like this before."

"You and your friends are doing the right thing." Mr. Shell smiled. "You'll be great!"

After breakfast, the Shells headed to the community center where the hearing was being held. Hundreds of animals had already gathered around with their own signs to save the beach. Snap was pleased to know the article served its purpose. As the moment came closer for him to speak, he felt the knot in his stomach get tighter and his head get lighter. He knew how important this speech was, and he also knew that if he was going to make a difference, everything had to be said perfectly.

A kind female pelican greeted Snap at the entrance and said he would speak after Mayor Crane gave his speech. Snap gulped after hearing the official agenda. He had never spoken in front of a public figure, like a mayor before. This could possibly be the biggest thing he had ever gotten himself into. Snap looked around and spotted all of his new friends starting to make their way inside. Tula ran up to Snap and gave him a hug. Lucas was right behind her.

"This is so awesome! You are so awesome, Snap! I can't wait to hear you speak!" Snap grinned as Tula wrapped her arms around his shell.

"We'll see if he can really pull this off. I have my doubts." Lucas laughed and nudged Tula's shoulder. Snap knew Lucas was just envious of his new popularity and tried to ignore his negative remarks. As all of the animals started to gather around and get seated, Snap found his place in the front row next to a seal who was busy taking notes.

After Mayor Crane was introduced and informed the audience of the benefits behind moving forward on the project, the kind looking pelican motioned for Snap to come forward. Snap looked around, hoping it wasn't already time to speak. How could he go right after the Mayor who just gave a speech about the benefits of building the roadway? Who was *he* to go against the Mayor? Snap realized he didn't have a choice, when the Pelican continued to stare directly at him while motioning for him to get up. Snap slowly stood up and walked to the front while clearing his throat a few times. She introduced him as a local party who would like to inform the residents of further information regarding Trestles. She gave him a wink, handed him the microphone and Snap took his spot at the podium.

Snap cleared his throat again into the microphone and fumbled with the speech he held in his hand. He could feel beads of sweat on his forehead, and for a moment, lost his balance. He positioned himself on his flippers and took a moment to breath in and out.

"Good Morning, My name is Snap Shell. I'm 10 years old and I live in Cardiff, California." Snap looked around at all of the eyes glued on him. He spotted Lucas with a smug look on his face, and immediately glanced toward Timmy who gave him a look of reassurance.

Morning Coffee Buzz

"I first wanted to say thank you for allowing me to speak. I'm representing the future generations that hopefully will help shape and protect our natural environment. There are many turtles and animals in California, America, and even all over the world that know what a special place Trestles is. It is home to the annual Surf Barrel Competition, which is now in its thirty-ninth year."

The silence was broken when Slide hollered out loud, "Woo Hoo! You tell 'em dude!"

Snap continued. *"The SWSHA represents a group of athletes who must make a B plus average in school to compete in this competition. This organization helps us strive to be better, and Trestles has been the home supporter for almost forty years."* Snap looked up from his paper and spotted Tula smiling in the crowd, next to Spike, Harry, and a few Hawksbills and Leatherbacks from surf school. No one was sitting with their normal groups, but mixed in all over the room. Snap's thoughts wandered off to Wrinklebutt for a second, and all of their talks flashed through his mind. After a moment, he found his spot and continued. *Oops.*

"Trestles is a jewel that must be protected. The experience of going to Trestles starts with the anticipation of surfing perfect waves in one of the most picturesque areas in southern California. As you go further down the path, the noise of the highway starts to disappear as you gaze out into the ocean. You emerge on the beach, and it is the same as the California coast that was there hundreds of years ago. You listen to the waves crash and rocks rumble as the waves wash across them. The waves in Trestles are some of the best waves in all of the United States and are also the top ten in the entire world.

Why are we even considering destroying a place that has been around since the beginning of time? This is one of the last unspoiled chunks of land on the coast in southern California. My friends and I have researched and have written an article published in yesterday's paper explaining all of the environmental damage this project will cause. It will not only directly impact the ecosystem and quality of the water, but will also cause toxins and oils to build up in the surrounding environment. The area is full of plants and endangered animals that will be harmed and get sick if we let this project happen. If we don't fight for a place like Trestles, what will be destroyed next?"

Snap paused, noticing the silence in the room and the echo from his microphone. He continued on, "We are the voices of future generations. Please do not allow this road to be built that will destroy over 60% of the park. I hope today I will always remember this day as the day Trestles was saved once and for all. Thank you for your time."[1]

The entire room stood up and began applauding and yelling for Snap. He walked down to meet his dad, who gave him a huge hug.

"I'm so proud of you, son. If that speech didn't save the beach, I don't know what will."

The pelican came over to Snap to congratulate him on a job well done. "We should know the decision by the end of the day, my dear boy. You'll be one of the first to be contacted." The pelican gave a confident nod to Snap's father, then walked away, pausing to take pictures between waves of her giant wings.

Snap walked out with his dad and friends by his side. All they could do now was wait, but what better way to pass the time than in the ocean? "Anyone up for some wave riding?" Snap yelled, and his entire surf class, minus Lucas, ran to get their boards.

With his father there on the shoreline, talking to an array of spectators, Snap and his friends hit the water of Pipes surf break. Snap threw in a few aerial tricks on Tula's request and even got

---

(1) Original speech written and presented by nine-year old Jake Marshall at the Del Mar Save Trestles-Stop the Toll Road Hearing in 2008 and rearranged and used with permission for the contents of this book.

Herbert to take a few snap shots for him to send to his best friend back home. Snap considered this day to be one of the best days of his life and wanted some pictures to capture the memories. Not only did he feel strong for giving such an important speech, but for the first time in Snap's entire life, his dad took the time to go to the beach and watch him surf. Today was a good day.

That night Snap got the much anticipated phone call from the mayor's office. It was Miss Pelican. "Snap, it's Penny P."

"Hi Miss P." He waited in silence on the phone.

"Good news, Snap. It is my honor to inform you that your speech created quite the stir in our department."

"That's good right?" Snap could feel the same old knot in his stomach come back.

"It's unbelievable! We had so many calls after the hearing, animals speaking out against the roadway, that the Mayor had no choice but to stop the project for further evaluation."

"Seriously?" Snap smiled, and nodded his head up and down.

"You saved the beach, Snap! You really did it! Surf Barrel 39 is still on!"

"Really? Thank you! I can't believe it! Thank you!" Snap was so excited he nearly fell over on his back.

"No, thank *you*. I was rooting for you the whole time. And by the way, Mayor Crane wanted me to send personal congratulations to you. He said that California needs more young and *wise* animals like you defending our beaches. He sees the whole project differently now because of *you*."

Snap couldn't believe what he heard. "This is totally sweet!" he yelled. This may have been the biggest moment of his life. He wished his mom were here to see him and that there was a way to share the news with Shelly. He thought about Tula and his best friend, Iggy. Before he notified anyone though, he ran downstairs to first tell his pops.

Star Says His First Word

CHAPTER 13

Timmy had Snap practicing air tricks non-stop at Wind n' Sea every evening the week before the competition. It was an exercise to build Snap's endurance. In the meantime, he was actually getting really good at his air reverse move. Timmy knew what it was like to need constant energy during a competition, so he worked Snap hard and asked him to be in bed by 8:00 PM every night. "Go home, eat a good meal, plenty of vegetables, get some rest, oh and lay off Turtle Tube," Timmy would say. Snap had spent so much time practicing and resting that he barely had time to spend with any of his new friends.

Two days before the competition, Snap was given a much needed surprise. Thursday afternoon after surf class, Snap was checking on the weather conditions in Trestles hour-by-hour when he received a knock at the door. He realized that he didn't call Tula back and she was probably coming by to either check on him or chew him out for ignoring her the past few days. *Oh Tula, not right now*, he thought.

Snap got up from his laptop and headed to the door.

He could hear a high pitch voice outside that sounded like a cross between Herbert and Tula. He couldn't tell for sure but thought they were both outside his door arguing.

When Snap opened the door, he literally had to catch his breath to swallow. "Iggy? Molly? What? What? What are you? Mr. Green? Mrs. Green?" Snap noticed the Greens had even brought their new addition to the family. "You brought the egg?"

In eagerness to get inside, Iggy fell into his best friend while his little sister pushed past them. Snap was so excited that he didn't know what to say. He just hugged his best friend and repeatedly

Star Says His First Word

said, "I can't believe it!" Snap's father came to the door after hearing all the commotion.

"Come on in, everyone!" Mr. Shell said.

Snap looked to his father. "Pops? You knew?"

"Yep. I knew you wouldn't want your best friend to miss your competition. And it was perfect timing. Mr. Green had a marathon to run in Carlsbad this weekend. So a few phone calls and some route planning, and here they are."

Iggy smiled at his friend and agreed. "Yep. Here we are."

Snap was so overjoyed and surprised that he didn't even know where to begin.

"You really do walk on two feet now?" Iggy patted Snap on the back shell. "I can't believe it. Wait till Lizibeth and the others hear about this."

"Why don't you go show Iggy around, Snap." Mr. Shell wanted to give the two boys some time to catch up.

"Hey! What about me? If you expect me to babysit that egg, I will never ever..."

"You can come too, Molly. I'll introduce you to Tula," Snap said.

"Who's Tula?" Iggy's sister asked. "Your *girlfriend?*"

Snap looked up at his father and said, "No!" He then nudged Iggy and said, "I'll introduce you to everyone!" Within a moment, the three of them were out the door. "Be back, Pops!"

Snap gave Iggy and Molly a history lesson of Turtle Town and even let Molly hold the map while he escorted them down to the beach.

"You know, this makes no sense to me. I'd rather color it," Molly said.

As they passed the Coaster, they spotted Tula, Spike and Lucas at the surf shop from across the street. "Perfect timing," Snap said. "You can meet Trek too. He's the lizard I told you about." Snap watched his best friend's eyes light up at that bit of news. "And he even swims under water!"

"How lovely," Molly smirked. She acted annoyed but became interested when she spotted Tula in her hot pink board skirt. "Look! It's Olive and a body builder!"

"No Molly, that's not Olive, it's Tula *and* Lucas!" Snap cringed as he watched Lucas hand something to Tula.

"Who's the crab?" Iggy asked.

"Come on, you'll see." Snap walked up to his friends and shared his surprise with them. Lucas ignored the iguanas and walked into the surf shop.

"That's my competition," Snap whispered to Iggy. "The guy I'm gonna beat at the surf competition."

"Seriously? That guy's in your age category?"

"Yep."

"He looks like someone's dad," Iggy said.

When Snap and the iguanas walked up to Tula, she instantly recognized them from the picture in Snap's bedroom. "Iggy and Molly, right?" She smiled.

"Why, yes, that is correct." Molly curtsied. She took an immediate liking to Tula and asked where she could get a matching pink skirt like hers.

"At the surf shop! Want me to take you?" Tula suggested.

Molly's attention drifted when she spotted Star. "What?! A sea star!" Molly ran up to Star, who was busy clinging to Herbert's back, and screamed with excitement. She reached down and peeled him right off Herbert's back.

Everyone stared in shock. No one had ever tried picking up Star before. The little starfish went into hysterics and started wiggling profusely in Molly's hand, so the little lizard squeezed him even tighter. "Oh, no you don't. You're mine now."

Star Says His First Word

Star bounced out of Molly's hand, leaving not one, but two of his limbs behind. Molly looked down at the leg and arm wiggling around in her palm and screamed, tossing the pieces to the ground.

"That's what you get!" Star screamed and cart-wheeled away.

"Did he just???" Spike spun around and looked at Herbert and back at Snap and then down at little Molly. "You just got Star to speak? I thought he was mute?"

"We all thought that," Tula said, and all of them, including Iggy, who had no idea what was happening, laughed.

"Molly, you really are something." Snap patted her on the head.

"What? What did I do?" She gave them all an "innocent" smirk.

Naturally, the entire group looked over at Herbert, whose mouth and claws were opened wide. He said nothing. Someone in the crowd said, "I think that's what they mean by shell-shock." Herbert pointed a claw at Molly with a look of horror and quickly scattered away after the three-legged starfish.

All of the animals went to the surf shop to say hello to Trekker and Timmy, and of course, buy Molly a pink board skirt. Lucas stormed out of the shop when they entered, nearly knocking everyone over. Snap looked over at Iggy and told him to ignore him. "We're all used to it now."

"Well, look who we have here?" *Phfff.* Trekker was happy to have a group full of visitors. "Did you bring a whole crew to help you sweep, Snap Snap?" *Phfff.* Trekker nudged Snap in the shoulder.

"No," Snap said. "And I didn't forget." Snap looked over at Iggy and said, "This is my best friend from back home, Iggy, and his little sister, Molly."

Molly didn't turn around because her attention was on the rack of pink skirts. "Likewise," she mumbled.

"Well, well. Your friend Iggy here would be a great candidate for a helmet or maybe even a foam board rental." *Phfff.*

"I just want a skirt." Molly smiled up toward Trekker and said, "What's wrong with your head?"

"Wrong?" *Phfff.* "Why, there's nothing wrong with my head," Trekker explained. He then went on to lay out the details of the peculiar device. "This little lady is the Sea Trek, and it happens to be one of the fastest growing underwater, fail-safe, microprocessor-controlled air delivery systems..."

Molly cut him off and mimicked him. *Phfff.*

"Is there something wrong with your nose, little lizard?" Trekker asked. *Phfff.*

Molly shook her head *no* and repeated the annoying sound. *Phfff.* She reached up and said she wanted to touch the helmet, and Trekker ignored her. "Alright, cutie. We'll get you fixed up in a pink board skirt so you can be on your way." *Phfff.*

Molly whipped her head back up when she heard Trekker make the sound again, but walked off to the girls apparel section with Tula.

Snap laughed, because he had always been a fan of Molly's humor. "So anyway, do you think I could take Iggy out for a ride?" Snap asked.

Iggy gave Snap a questioning look.

"You said you did it once in Jamaca, right?"

"Well, I didn't exactly get up, but sure, why not." Iggy showed a little tension in his half smile.

"What if you use a body board? It's easier," Snap said.

Timmy came around from the back with a can of *Tur-tle Wax*.

"Timmy! This is Iggy! I've told him all about you."

"Sweet, dude," Timmy said. "I hear you want to take him out, brah?"

Star Says His First Word

"Yeah. He just needs a board."

Timmy grabbed a body board for Iggy, and all of the reptiles followed him down to the shore. "How about you show him a few moves on your new board, brah?"

So he did notice the new board, Snap thought. Snap wanted to tell Timmy the story about Wrinklebutt and her hide out, but his intuition told him that Timmy probably knew already. Maybe he was keeping her secret too.

Snap went out into the ocean to show his best friend what he'd been up to since he arrived to the West Coast. After warming up, Snap did a few air reverses to show off for his friends and rode the wave all the way in.

"Wow! You're so good!" Iggy clapped. "It looks hard, though."

"It's a workout." Snap grabbed Iggy's board and handed it to him.

"Well. You look like you're in really good shape. I meant to tell you."

Snap had probably lost a few pounds and gained some muscles from his daily workouts, and it was apparent to his friend who hadn't seen him in some time.

"So, you ready?" Snap asked.

Iggy bit his lip and nodded.

"Let's go!"

Snap and Iggy spent a few hours in the water while Tula helped Molly build a sand castle on the beach.

After Iggy's tail got tangled in the Pacific seaweed one time too many, he was ready for a break and some grub. "That was more tiring than baseball." Iggy fell down to his knees in the sand right in front of Molly's sand castle.

"Hey, watch it!" Molly yelled. *Phffffffff!*

Everyone played together for a while before Timmy called out to Snap, reminding him he needed to get some rest before the competition. That night, the Shell's, the Green's, Tula, Spike, Trekker and Timmy all had dinner at Snap's house. Iggy's mom offered to cook her famous veggie lasagna. Iggy told a joke and reminded everyone it was *famous* because she always managed to burn it no matter how long she left it in the oven. After an entire evening of board games, everyone went home, except the Greens. They stayed in the guest bedroom, and Snap made Iggy a bed on the floor in his room out of sleeping bags and bean bags.

"I can't believe I'm here! California!" Iggy sighed and fell into his pillow. "You should have seen the look on your face when you opened the door this morning."

"I know, man. I was totally shocked!" They talked for a while longer, about the beach, Wrinklebutt, the competition and Tula, of course. Iggy wanted to know all about her.

"Will we see her tomorrow?" Iggy asked.

Star Says His First Word

"Maybe," Snap yawned. He knew he had to wake up early to get his competition number, shirt and rules for Surf Barrel 39, so after a few more minutes of chatting, both reptiles fell asleep.

Chapter 14
No One is As They Seem

The next morning, Snap rolled out of bed, trying to avoid Iggy and his long tail on the floor.

"Hey. Where are you going?" The iguana stretched and turned to Snap, who was now washing his face in the connecting bathroom.

"I told you last night, dude. I gotta catch the Coaster to go get all of my stuff up north for the competition tomorrow."

"Coaster?" the iguana questioned.

"Yeah, man. The train…"

"I wanna go on a train."

"I thought you would. Then come on and get up, sleepyhead. I'll be downstairs getting our snacks ready."

Snap grabbed a few items for the two of them to snack on and let his dad know they were leaving soon. While he waited for Iggy to come downstairs, the box shell turtle stood on the front porch for a moment and felt confident, knowing that no matter what happened in the competition, he would have the most important animals there by his side to support him.

"Ready?" Iggy came through the front door to meet Snap.

"Yeah, man. Just waiting on you to finish getting pretty."

"Hey! Just combing my spines." Iggy retorted.

"Just kidding. Let's go." Snap handed Iggy a granola bar.

When Snap and Iggy arrived at the train station, they found Harry, Lucas and a few other Leatherbacks already there."

"Surprise, surprise. So you didn't chicken out, eh?" Lucas laughed.

Snap ignored his comment and gave Harry a head nod.

"Hey, look!" Iggy tapped Snap's shell. "Tula's coming."

Snap turned around to see Tula walking up to the train station. "Hey, guys." She waved and smiled at Iggy.

"Tula? What are you doing here?" *She really didn't have to go all the way up north with me*, he thought to himself, but he was flattered she had come to meet him, even if he didn't want to admit it.

Tula started fidgeting with her bracelets. That's when Snap noticed she was acting sort of strange. *Wait a second,* he thought. He glanced at Lucas, who was grinning directly at Tula.

"Yeah, Tu-Tu," Lucas balked, as soon as Snap whipped his head back to Tula. "Why don't you tell him what you're doing here, anyway," Lucas snickered as the train pulled up to pick them up. The turtles got on, and Snap watched as Tula hesitated on her decision of where to sit. After their conversation on his balcony the other night, Snap figured Tula would have no problem sitting with him on the train. She finally took a seat directly across from Snap and Iggy. He took that as a good sign, or so he thought.

"Seriously, though. What's going on, Tula?" Snap was becoming a bit concerned by her awkward attitude, even though he knew her to have her moods.

Tula pulled a piece of paper out of her shell and set it on the seat next to him. Snap quickly grabbed the paper and realized what it was.

What? "You're competing in Surf Barrel? Against me? But how?" Snap was shocked.

"It's co-ed. I can surf too," Tula said in defense.

"I know. It's just, you didn't tell me. How long did you know you were going to compete?"

Tula sat there for a moment with a sad expression. "I signed up when you were away with Wrinklebutt."

Snap immediately cut her off. "Shhh. Don't say that so loud," he huffed. "So you knew this whole time, and you didn't say anything? During the hearing, on my balcony, last night with my family and friends?" Snap turned to Iggy to get some support. Iggy shrugged.

"I'm sorry, Snap. I just didn't know how to tell you, so I kept putting it off."

"But you had plenty of chances. *This* is how you wanted me to find out?"

Tula put her head down. Snap knew she had more to say. "And well, Lucas kinda talked me into it."

"What?" Snap was confused. He looked around the train to see if Lucas was watching their whole conversation. No sign of him. He wasn't on the train. *Weird.*

"You were gone!" She whipped her head back up.

"So? Lucas? I mean, Lucas? What does he have to do with anything you're doing?"

Tula turned her attention back toward Snap. "What's the big deal about Lucas? Why are you always so worried about him, dude?"

"What?! You were the one who called him a creaton! Don't act like I'm dumb, Tula." Snap tried to keep his voice down on the train. "I know he gave you *both* of those bracelets!" He paused, waiting for her response, but she kept quiet so he continued, "I've noticed him hanging around you lately. Don't you see what he's doing? He's using you to get to me."

Tula still didn't respond. She acted like she was watching the scenery out the window as the train pulled north.

"You were right all along, Tula." Snap crossed his arms and leaned back in his seat.

"About what?" She peaked up with water in her eyes.

"No one really *is* as they seem here. It didn't take that long for me to learn that. You can't trust *anyone* here." Snap looked at her, then at the seat behind him to make sure no one was listening and said, "Not even you." He folded his arms and turned his body to one side, facing the window so she couldn't see his face.

The three reptiles sat in silence the rest of the ride up north. Snap had never felt so betrayed. He thought about their time together and the secrets he shared with her, and he wondered now if perhaps she may have shared them with Lucas. Once the train came to a stop, Snap rushed off to get to the Surf Barrel tent before the others. Iggy ran behind him. Snap was pretty fast on two feet, especially when he was angry. He barged straight to the yellow and black stand.

"Last name?" A big Leatherback with aviator shades asked from behind the Surf Barrel table.

"Shell."

"Snap Shell?" He pointed at Snap's name with his pen.

"Yes."

"Here yah go, B.T." The Leatherback smirked.

"Thanks." Snap grimaced and grabbed his blue shirt and number. "Come on." Snap motioned for his friend to follow. They rushed passed Tula in the opposite direction and hurried back to catch the next train. He didn't want to be on the same train as her going back. Snap and Iggy were the only ones on the otherwise empty train. He couldn't help but replay the conversation he had with Tula on his balcony. Tula told him that she missed him, and she realized when he was gone how good of a friend he was to her. How could she say that to him after hanging out with Lucas all week? Now she had gone behind Snap's back to enter the competition, and even worse, she did it because of Lucas' suggestion. How could he ever trust her again? How could he trust anyone?

"Are you okay?" Iggy asked, breaking the silence.

Snap huffed and looked across the seat to his friend. "How could she?"

"I know, Snap. I mean..." he paused and thought for a moment, "I kinda know how you feel."

"You mean with Liz?" Snap remembered last year when he had given Iggy advice on how to handle his problems. Snap used to always give Iggy advice, and now he was hoping his friend had some in return.

"Honestly, Snap, if it was me, and you were giving me advice, you would say that I am going to have to forgive her."

Snap sat there questioning if that's what he would have said.

"Come on, Snap. It's not like she stole your board, or worse, your necklace."

Snap looked at his friend, gritting his teeth when he talked. "But it's trust, man. Trust is everything in a friendship. You know that," Snap sighed and started wringing his hands in worry.

"I know. I'm just trying to make sure you don't lose her as a friend. Maybe she needs someone like you in her life to help her change."

"But it's just, *she* keeps changing on *me*! I never know what to expect from her. She acts like she is my friend one minute and then the next, she's someone else." Snap shook his head, "But what's worse is that she started hanging out with Lucas again behind my back." Snap thought about the paper Lucas had given Tula just yesterday.

"I know how you feel. Liz and I are just starting to get back to normal again." Iggy went through the same thing with Buddy the bullfrog back in fourth grade who was picking on him, and of course, Snap had been there for Iggy.

"I just don't know how I'm going to feel tomorrow at the competition." The Coaster stopped, and the two reptiles got off at Solana Beach to head back to Cardiff for Snap's last practice with Timmy.

"I don't get it, though," Iggy scratched his head. "Why would Lucas want Tula to compete against him too? Didn't you say she's actually pretty good?"

"Yeah. You're right," Snap paused and crinkled his brow, "I don't know, but he's definitely up to something. That I know for sure, dude," he sighed. "Did you notice that Lucas wasn't even on the train earlier?"

"No way...but he was at the station!"

Both reptiles headed down to the beach. Snap continuing to replay Tula's words, *no one here is as they seem*. He wondered if that meant everyone, Trekker, Timmy, Herbert, Star...When they got to the beach, Snap was surprised to see every single animal he had ever come across, plus some others gathered around the shoreline to watch his final practice with Timmy.

"Wow! You're like *famous* around here," Iggy gasped. "Does it always look like this?"

"Not quite." Snap gazed around the beach scene. It looked like a festival. A few turtles had even set up tents. Some of the Olive Ridley bale came up to wish Snap luck. Barney was even wearing a button with Snap's face on it.

"Hey, man. Where did you get that?"

Barney pointed down to the surf shop where Herbert was running a lemonade stand and selling Snap Shell buttons.

No One is As They Seem

"Did you ask him to do that?" Iggy pointed toward Herbert's stand.

"Nope."

"I think it's kinda cool," Iggy said.

"Herbert must have come up with the business idea all on his own. Marketing." Snap had no clue that he would become a Turtle Town celebrity before he even competed. He started to worry whether his fan club would diminish tomorrow if he didn't win and move on to the Hawaiian Nationals.

"You sure do draw attention, little buddy." Timmy patted Snap on the shell and handed him some wax for his board.

"I had no idea it would be this big of a deal." Snap looked around the beach forgetting his previous concerns. D.J. Slide was spinning a disc and had the music playing loud, while Mossy passed out Surf Barrel flyers to all the young turtles playing on the beach. He had even shaved the moss off his face for the occasion.

"Yep. Pretty unreal. Wait until you go pro," Timmy said with a smile.

"Come on, Tim. I'm only ten." Snap followed Timmy out into the water, and Iggy found Trekker over at the lemonade stand.

Snap reached for his necklace while he paddled out into the swell. He knew he wouldn't be able to wear it tomorrow. He wasn't going to go back on his word, even if Lucas was trying everything in his flippers to sabotage Snap's chance to win.

Snap was able to stay focused while in the water, and his rides proved to be excellent. He looked strong. He rode smooth. His tricks were firm and in rhythm. He practiced going through the motions, at a slower than competitive pace, and gave the entire audience a preview of what was to come.

When the practice session was over, Timmy offered him some final words of encouragement. A group of spectators gathered around Snap as he left the water and patted him on the back, telling him how wonderful he was. Snap couldn't believe it was all happening. He actually forgot all about Tula and Lucas at that moment. He glanced over at his friend, Iggy, who flew all the way from Texas to see him, and he thought about how far he had come. A few months ago, he was worried about winning a summer All Star baseball game back in Texas. A few weeks ago he was worried about maintaining his balance on two feet, and today he was strong enough to not only surf, but bring marine life together for a good cause. This final ride on the water helped him regain his confidence and helped him focus on his one important friend, Iggy. Snap worried that the popularity of the occasion would get to his head, but his friend helped him keep things in perspective.

At dinner that evening, Snap and his father, along with the Greens, sat together at the table and ate and talked about things besides surfing. Snap didn't say too much. He tried really hard to take in the moment and enjoy their friends.

Later that night, Snap had a dream that outdid all of his other dreams since moving to California.

His mother was competing in his place for him. Snap was in the crowd, and his mother was wearing his blue shirt and his number—three. The waves turned black, as black as oil. His mother had already gone out for her third set, and there was no turning back. Everyone on the beach was in awe of the sky that had also turned black as night. Lightning cracked, and Snap noticed that his mom was the only surfer out in the ocean. The announcers called off the competition due to dangerous weather. Snap started to yell. "Wait, my mom is out there! Wait, my mom is out there!" Sirens started going off, and no one could hear Snap's cries. "Please, someone help her. Anyone! Help her!" The sirens rang and seemed to drown out all sound from around the ocean and the beach.

That's when Snap awoke from his sleep and hit his alarm buzzer. He looked around and could feel the sweat dripping down his neck into his shell.

What time is it? Snap looked over as his friend started sitting up. Iggy got up off the floor, cracked his back, and sat on the end of Snap's bed.

"Bad dream?" Iggy asked in a crackling voice.

"Yeah," Snap said. "I think so. But it was just a dream." Snap took off his necklace and set it on his nightstand. He rolled out of bed and got into the shower without saying another word to Iggy.

The house buzzed with energy that morning, as all of the reptiles in the house had somewhere to be. The Greens were heading to Carlsbad for the marathon, except for Iggy who was going with the Shells to the surf competition.

Mr. Shell packed up the car with lawn chairs, snacks, binoculars and a few signs Molly made as a surprise while Snap and Iggy were gone yesterday.

When they arrived at Trestles beach, Iggy spotted Tula walking in their direction. "Um, Snap," Iggy said without moving his lips.

Snap was in the zone, focusing on what was to come and didn't notice her.

"Um, Snap," Iggy said once more.

"Huh?"

"Tula."

Snap looked up only seconds before she was right in front of him. "Hi." Tula said, quietly.

Oh man. "Hi."

Noticing the awkwardness, Iggy told Snap he was going to help his pops set up. Snap obviously needed to speak to Tula alone. Snap watched as Iggy turned and walked up the beach.

"Sorry," Tula said once Iggy was out of earshot. "I'm a bit nervous."

"Me too."

"Well, did you hear what happened?" she asked.

"Hear what?" Snap hadn't heard any news in the past 24 hours.

"About Lucas?"

"No. What happened?" Snap's eyes grew wide.

"He's out."

What? "Of the competition? How?"

"His seventh grade teacher from last year told Timmy that he failed math last year. Lucas forged his grades to get to compete. He thought he would get away with it."

Snap's jaw dropped. "No one told me."

"I know."

"Wait," Snap started. "Is that why he told you to compete? Actually, let me guess, you already knew that too, huh?"

"No, Snap, I had no idea." She reassured him and looked him straight in the eyes. "But it all makes sense now." She untied the bracelets on her wrists and threw them in the sand. "You were right. He was using me."

Snap started rubbing his neck. "This is awful!" He stomped away, leaving Tula by herself. He gritted his teeth and spoke to himself where no one could hear him, not even Tula. Just when he was ready to prove himself to Lucas, his chance was ruined. Here he was emotionally ready to prove to Lucas he was as good a surfer as any sea turtle on the beach, especially one who bullied him around, and he's not even competing. His only real competition was a girl he really liked, who proved to him that she was nothing more than an ex-good friend. Snap started having difficulty getting his thoughts together and focusing on the competition. He knew he had to find a way to regain his balance, his emotional focus, or the entire reason he wanted to compete would be in vain.

Chapter 15

Sara Shell

Snap went to gather his thoughts near a patch of palms away from the crowds. He didn't need anyone to witness his outburst. It was better for him to gain his composure in private. Well, if he were ever in private.

"Snap," said a voice from behind a sand mound. Snap turned to find Wrinklebutt hiding out to watch the surf competition.

"Shelly? You came?" Snap was relieved to find her there. He knew that her presence, not to mention her words, could calm him down.

"You're bothered, Snap. What's happened to make you upset?" Shelly came out from behind the sand mound.

Snap knew if he told Shelly how angry he was about Lucas getting kicked out of the competition and Tula being his new competitor she would come back with some peaceful series of questions to search deep into Snap's soul. All he really wanted was to kick a tree and Lucas' back shell, for that matter. But he had no choice but to be honest with her.

Snap listed out the details of all the things that were upsetting him, and after listening to his dilemma, Wrinklebutt said, "So yet again, this is still about the necklace."

"What?" Did she not hear him mention the competition not going his way? That he would be competing against a girl, but not just any girl, Tula. "How is this about the necklace?"

Wrinklebutt had an encouraging look on her face and waited for him, knowing he would figure it out for himself. She patiently gave him time to think.

When Snap paused to recollect his thoughts, he realized, it *was* about the necklace.

"What have I told you about the *O'ia'o* symbol?"

"I've gotta stay true to myself to find myself," Snap said slowly.

"Right. Your spirit is strong, Snap. Don't fear. Just go out there and satisfy your spirit, no one or nothing else. Remember, you are the reason all of these animals are here surfing today," she reminded him.

"I couldn't have done it alone." Snap looked around at the hundreds, maybe thousands of animals with signs and horns who had come for the competition. He realized that beyond the signs, the announcer, the fans, the surfboards or waves, this moment had nothing to do with the actual spirit of surfing. It was up to him to decide why he was really there.

"Okay, Shelly. I think I get it this time. Honest," Snap said looking her directly in the eyes. He wanted her to know he really did mean it. She returned his look with a smile, and as the pair stood face to face, Snap watched a shadow begin to form across her forehead. He looked up at the sky and saw a dark patch of clouds moving in from the south.

Snap's mentor looked up to the sky and said, "It's the best time to surf." She patted him on the head and walked away saying, "I'll be watching."

A breeze blew across Snap's head, sending a chill down his shell as he watched Shelly walk back behind the sand mounds. The moment felt surreal, like he was back in a dream. Again, he was by himself, but he continued to look up at the sky and couldn't help but think and wonder, *was he really alone?* "This is for you, mom," he said under his breath.

Snap walked up to the announcer stand to check-in. The Leatherback checked his name and gave him an odd look while looking down at his blue flippers.

"Tortoise?" he questioned.

Snap flipped his visor around backward and said, "Reptile." He walked away feeling confident and proud of himself and found his pops and Iggy.

"Where did you go?" Iggy asked.

"Just needed to clear my head."

"Everything okay, son?" Mr. Shell asked.

"Yep." Snap answered with few words.

"Hey, Snap!" He turned to find Herbert and Star, Trekker, and the entire Olive Ridley bale, minus Tula and Spike, coming up to wish him luck.

"I don't quite believe in luck, as luck is just a mere chance, but anyhow, good luck, *Monsieur* Snap Shell." Herbert bowed, and Star jumped off Herbert's back and onto Snap's shell.

"Rip it up, man!" Slide gave Snap a fist bump.

Snap noticed Spike give Tula some last words a few yards away from his support group. Snap couldn't believe that they both weren't a part of each other's big moment. He tried to push the thought out of his mind. It was time for his division to begin.

"Welcome to the Surf Barrel 39 Junior Co-Ed Open Division! Surfers! Please check in five minutes before your heat," the announcer yelled.

Snap turned to his dad and said, "I'm glad you're here, Pops."

"I'll always be here for you, son," Mr. Shell replied.

Snap joined Timmy, who had gathered his students together to explain the last minute rules. "Okay, so you know they are taking the top three out of each heat."

Everyone in the group nodded, yes.

Timmy looked up at the sky and breathed in the air while smiling. "I love a good storm."

Snap looked back up to the sky. The clouds had already turned to a dark grey. A raindrop hit Snap's wrist. As long as there was no lightning, the competition would go on. He looked over at Tula in her red shirt. She looked ready, considering everything that had happened. Harry was in green, and he looked pretty good too. Snap looked down at his blue shirt and then at the other three turtles in his heat, all Leatherbacks.

Timmy signaled for everyone to run out to the water, but held Snap back for a second to say one last thing to his special student.

"It's all about you, Snap. No one else. Don't forget that."

"Thanks, Timmy. I got it now." Snap nodded and ran out into the ocean with his board. He thought about the first time he had surfed the sea, the times back in Texas when he told everyone he was going to be a surfer, and now, he had the opportunity of a lifetime to prove it. He just needed to stay in the right mindset, the mindset he had during his week with Wrinklebutt.

Sara Shell

As soon as the water hit Snap's blue flippers and rushed to his ankles, he felt the comfort of the ocean. He felt in his heart he was right where he belonged. No, he wasn't an aquatic turtle, but if he had learned anything in his experiences in this strange new world of California or alone with Wrinklebutt, he learned that everyone was unique in their own way yet similar to everything around them. All the insecurities he faced when he first arrived to Turtle Town subsided as the sea swelled around his shell.

The waves had already started to grow in size, which only exhilarated his senses. *It all comes down to this,* he thought. Snap knew the challenge was inside of him, not on the outside. He went farther out into the big waves of Lowers and pictured Wrinklebutt's beautiful shell and the mythological stories he heard about her life. He tried to imagine what she felt like in her first competition. His thoughts drifted from Wrinklebutt to his mother and all the times they watched the waves come into the shore, crashing against the buoys in Galveston Beach. He remembered the serenity that came with storms out on the ocean. Suddenly, right this moment, everything about the sea represented love—love between him and his mother, the love between him and Wrinklebutt, love between his father and friends who waited on the beach to support his dream.

As he pushed onward through the waves, he imagined how great his mother must have been in her first Surf Barrel competition and how nervous she must have felt being so different from the sea turtles. For a split second, the sun seemed to peek through the clouds. He felt calm and confident, at peace with the storm that quickly swallowed the sunlight. Snap realized he had found his inner puka.

Snap rubbed his bare neck one last time and looked down at the symbol on his board. He focused on it, meditating on the connection between him and his mother. *Wait,*

Snap thought. Between the splashes of water and the rolling waves he noticed something else on the board. Snap inspected a bit closer and realized, there *was* more. He peeled with his nails and realized, there, buried beneath layers of board wax was another engraving:

S. Shell Surf Barrel 29

"WHAT?" Snap yelled. *Mom's board?* For a moment, he panicked and looked around the water to see if somehow Wrinklebutt was in the water with him. Snap's mother's name was Sara Shell, and immediately he wondered if somehow she still placed at Surf Barrel, even after the accident. Everything made sense to him now. Snap knew why Shelly knew the exact board to give to him. He touched his neck where his necklace would have been and then paddled harder and stronger. He was ready to ride this wave with everything inside his shell.

The heat of six surfers had thirteen minutes to ride and get in their top two best scores. Snap didn't stall and went straight for the first big wave he felt coming. He pushed and pulled and lifted himself on the board, feeling a rush of adrenaline as he ripped his wave rail to rail.

The announcer yelled over the loud speaker, *"It's going off out there! Ten footers for sure. Opening score for surfer in blue, 7.1!"*

Snap got out of the water, looking for his coach's approval. Timmy was standing out in the middle of the beach, and from a distance, gave him a thumbs-up. Snap returned the gesture and ran back to the starting spot to go in for his next set.

Back on the beach, Mr. Shell and Iggy looked at each other and back at Timmy to see if the score was considered high. The thumbs up he returned to them was a good sign.

Sara Shell

"Pretty gnarly for a box shell. Jim, have you ever seen a box shell surf?" The announcer asked over the loud speaker.

"Not since Surf Barrel 29. That didn't go too well, though," the other announcer chuckled.

Mr. Shell growled under his breath, knowing they were talking about Sara Shell.

"Opening score for surfer in red, 6.8 and surfer in green 7.0."

Tula and Harry were keeping up.

Snap hopped back up for his second but almost got knocked down by a drop-in Leatherback in yellow. "Hey, man! My wave," he yelled.

"*Interference yellow on blue!*" The announcer yelled.

Snap got back up on his board and eyed Tula, who was already riding her second wave in. He went back out to catch his set. He looked down at the writing engraved on his board and thought about his mother. *I can do it.* He started to believe he could actually win this contest.

Snap took a wave far to the right, cutting it back and forth out of its barrel, scoring a 7.3 on his second wave. He wasn't sure how much time was left, but he had to catch a few more waves in case the other competitors were scoring high at their end.

Harry, Tula, and Snap all took advantage of the same set, but worked to keep out of each other's way.

"Alright, let me give you the situation out in the water, third wave coming in for surfer in green, 6.9, surfer in red, 3.9, surfer in yellow 5.1, and surfer in blue 6.8. Surfer in green needs a 6.8 to advance into first. Wearing the heat, surfer in blue!"

Mr. Shell and Iggy looked at each other with confused looks. Timmy turned around and yelled, "That means he's in first place. He's wearing the heat!"

"Yea! Go Snap!" Iggy yelled and held up his sign. Below them, they heard a tiny French accent applauding Snap's efforts as Star threw his arms together to clap for Snap.

"*Five minutes remaining in the heat,*" the announcer yelled.

Snap noticed the waves getting heavier on his fourth and fifth rides, and they grew higher than ten feet for the first time in the competition. The air grew cold as the sky continued to darken. A few of the surfers were wading out on their boards, taking a rest. Snap looked over to Tula and noticed she looked tired as the waves thrashed her back and forth. He started to get concerned for her, knowing she was a bit small for big wave riding, but he said nothing. There was no telling Tula what to do.

Snap looked up at the sky, which had now turned completely black, and he wondered if the competition would make it all the way through before the thunder and lightning moved in. The waves roared so loudly it was hard to hear the announcers, much less the applauding from the fans out on the beach. The darker the sky became and the higher the waves grew, Snap's confidence began to subside into fear.

Time was almost up, so he hurried to get in his final set. When he turned around to catch his last wave, he noticed Tula had the same plan and was already paddling forward in front of him. He stopped to let her have it. The wave grew into a monstrosity, forming a wall so high in front of Snap that he couldn't tell if Tula was riding in its barrel or if it rode over her. The wave seemed to keep growing and moving that when it finally broke, Snap couldn't see Tula anywhere. *Did she catch it? Did she catch it?* Snap looked toward the shore, between heavy splashes of water, but he couldn't see her. The rain started to come down, and it was getting almost impossible for him to see anything.

"No way!" Snap panicked and whipped his head to the right, then to the left, looking for the other four surfers. He didn't see anyone. *Did they all go under? Were they back on the beach? Was everyone quitting the competition?* He didn't know what he should do. He looked at the shore trying to figure out what was going on. He thought he saw Timmy running toward the water. Snap focused on the beach as hard as he could until he was certain it *was* Timmy.

Back on the beach Timmy was shouting "No! No! Tula!"

Please God, let her be okay, Snap thought. "Tula!" Snap yelled out to the ocean, and as soon as he did, a piece of Tula's pink and white board hit him in the side of his shell. *Her board,* he thought. "No!" he yelled again and started paddling toward the shore. The waves had broken her board in half. The waves grew and grew and pushed Snap up and down, making it almost impossible for him to see out in front of himself. He took in a deep breath and dove under the water to see if he could catch a glimpse of Tula, and just as he did, another part of her board hit him in the head. He came up for air, breathed in again and went back under.

He felt she had to be close to him, somewhere directly below him. Nothing mattered to him at that moment, not their arguments, not the competition, and especially not winning. All that mattered to Snap was finding his friend.

When Snap came back up again for air, out of the corner of his eye, Snap spotted Harry ride past him. How could he be riding at a time like this? Didn't he know Tula was in trouble?

Snap started to panic, questioning if he would even be able to make it back to shore. All of a sudden, something else slammed against Snap's shell. *Ouch*! Surely, it couldn't have been another piece of her board. Snap ignored the pain in his back shell and tried to remain focused. *Seriously dude, if one more thing hits me in the shell,* he thought. Then, to his surprise, he saw something that made him gain back all of his strength. It was Tula. "Tula!" He yelled. She was floating with her face down in the ocean. Snap grabbed her by her back shell, pulled her to him and laid her across his board. "Tula!" He started screaming in her ear, trying to yell over the roars of the ocean, but she just lay there motionless. Lifeless. "Tula! We have to get you back. I'll take you back. You'll be okay. Breathe Tula, breathe!" He repeated the words to her, and to himself, as he pulled himself and the board as hard as he could back toward the shore.

Snap wrestled the waves, and it seemed for every foot forward, the ocean sucked him back two times that distance. He pulled and paddled until his strength was just starting to give out. He clung to the surfboard as tightly as he could, and just before letting go from exhaustion, two huge turtle shells emerged above the water on both sides of him. Between choked gargles of water, Snap said, "Timmy? Shelly? You came!" One of them grabbed Tula on top of Snap's board, and the other grabbed him. Snap started to cry in relief, not only from the pain of the struggle, but the feeling of security knowing he and his friend might be okay.

Timmy held on tight to Snap's board while Wrinklebutt took Tula's face in her flippers and blew directly into her nose holes. "Come now, Tula. Wake up." Wrinklebutt then set her flipper across the little turtle's forehead, and this, time blew into her face. The little Olive Ridley started coughing up water. "You're okay. You're okay." Wrinklebutt repeated in a calming and soothing voice. "It's going to be okay."

Tula coughed and rubbed her eyes, trying to focus. "Wrinklebutt?" she questioned as she coughed up more salt water. Snap held Tula's flipper. "Snap?"

"It's me, Tula." Snap cried and coughed as he spoke to her with relief.

"Snap and Tim are going to take you back to the beach, Tula." Wrinklebutt said and nodded at Snap.

"We'll take you, Tula. It's going to be okay." Snap assured her.

"Promise?" she said.

"Yes, I promise. Everything will be okay."

"I meant with us."

Snap smiled and said nothing, reserving his energy for the final swim back to the shore. He held onto her flipper as tightly as he could to let her know he meant everything he said. Snap turned to look for Wrinklebutt, but she was nowhere to be found. Under his breath, Snap said, "Shelly?"

"Come on, brah. Let's get her to shore," Timmy said, grabbing the side of the board that Tula was lying on. Together, Timmy and Snap paddled back to shore with the board between them.

As they swam in, it suddenly hit Snap that he had given up his last ride and probably got outnumbered by either the surfer in yellow or Harry. It didn't matter anymore as he looked at the little Olive Ridley on his surfboard. He almost lost someone way more important than a competition. For the first time in his life, he knew exactly what his Pops must have felt ten years ago. Snap was just thankful that he could swim, and after all the practice, he was strong enough to withstand the waves that fought against him.

Once they hit sand, Timmy and some of the spectators helped carry her in. Snap collapsed beside her as more and more animals crowded around the scene. He worked to catch his breath.

Mr. Shell pushed his way toward his son with Iggy following closely behind him. "Son!" Mr. Shell fell to his knees, wrapped his arms around Snap, and held him tightly. "Oh, my," his father said between heavy sobs. "I thought I lost you, too!"

The experience of practically drowning had taken a lot out of Snap. He barely said a word to anyone as he continued to catch his breath. All he could do was motion to his father to check on Tula. "Make sure," he breathed in, "she's okay."

A few moments later, the sound of the waves was merged with the sound of sirens blaring as the medics pushed their way toward the beach. Spike sprinted to the group, tripping over turtle shells to get to his sister. "Tula. Are you okay?" He looked at Snap and said, "I owe you dude."

Snap held onto his pops and looking over his father's shoulder, he reached for Tula's flipper. Iggy knelt down next to Snap and Mr. Shell. "Snap. I'm so glad you're okay."

By this time, some of the competition officials began to push the crowd backward, asking for more room so the paramedics could work.

Snap noticed how tired Tula looked as she laid her head down in the sand. "It's going to be okay, Tula," animals kept repeating.

Tula tried to say something back, but her words were a faint whisper. Snap leaned his ear close to her mouth to hear what she was trying to say.

"We got to see Wrinklebutt."

Snap smiled. A ray of light shone down on Tula, and Snap followed the beam, looking up to the sky. The storm had already moved toward the north, and the sun peaked through one of the storm clouds. Suddenly, the sky lit up as if nothing had ever happened.

She tried to say something else, and again, Snap couldn't hear her.

"What was that, Tula? I'm right here," Snap said.

"Did you," she paused and coughed, "win?"

"Win? Me? Um, no, I don't think ..."

Just then, the announcer came over the loud speaker and told the crowd that Tula was going to pull through just fine. The audience applauded, and the announcers then continued by letting everyone know as soon as things settled down that they would finish the competition. *"Moving on to Open Mens! Surfers checking in."*

Snap Shell's heart was pounding in anticipation of the announcement and the results from the competition.

"Now for the results of the last heat," the announcer said. *"So, it looks like surfer in red is going to be okay thanks to surfer in blue. Way to be a hero!!!"* The announcer yelled. *"The final scores for the heat are coming in."*

Snap held his breath when he realized this was it. His pops moved in closer to him and put one hand on his son's shell. Iggy moved in as well, and with a look, let his friend know he was with him, no matter what.

Snap looked around before the results were announced and smiled as he made eye contact with each of his new friends, Trekker with his crazy space helmet, Herbert with his pseudo-French accent, Star with his crazed coffee habit, Spike, Iggy, and his instructor, Timmy. Lastly, he looked down at Tula who was smiling back at him. It seemed everything was going to be over as quickly as it began. He wasn't sure he stood a chance, and in his mind, Snap convinced himself he would try again next year.

"The winner of the Junior Co-Ed open and moving on to the Hawaiian Nationals is ..."

Just then, Tula squeezed Snap's hand, and Mr. Shell patted his son on the back for luck.

"Surfer in blue with a 7.2! Second goes to surfer in green with a 7.18! And third goes to surfer in yellow with a 6.86!"

Snap's mouth opened, and his eyes widened as Tula started to cheer between coughs, "You won, Snap. You won!"

"What? How?" Snap said. *Me?*

*"*This year's winner is none other than the little box shell turtle from Texas!"

"You gave up your score, and you still won!" Tula lifted herself up to wrap her arms around Snap.

Snap couldn't believe it. He only beat Harry by .02 points. He sat on the ground with nothing to say, and before he knew it, all his new friends were cheering, patting him on his shell, and applauding.

"Go up to get your new surf board, brah." Timmy pulled Snap off the ground.

Snap gave Timmy a high five and he proudly went up to receive his trophy and brand new *Tortuga* Board, with each of his friends following behind him. When Snap reached the podium, he turned to wave to all his friends, and he became teary-eyed when he saw not only his pops, but Herbert crying. He held the surfboard above his head for everyone to see. He couldn't believe it was really happening.

He ran his finger along the engraving, which read *Surf Barrel 39* across the nose. If only his mom could have been there to see him now. In between the cheers and pats on the shell, Snap looked past the crowd into the ocean, and somehow, deep inside himself, he knew Wrinklebutt and his mom were watching.

Trekker invited the whole gang up to the surf shop for snow cones and bowls of berries and kelp, and all of them gathered together to talk about the amazing surfing and of course, the amazing rescue. The entire evening, Tula stayed close to Snap, hardly ever leaving his side. Snap couldn't help but wonder if Lucas somehow got to see the competition. He knew his days of competing against Lucas weren't over. No way the Leatherback would back down that easily.

The next morning, Snap woke up bright and early, not to go surfing, but to take a stroll on the beach. He ran into Herbert and Star outside the coffee shop.

"Morning, *monsieur*!" Herbert said in a bow. "Have you seen the new billboard?"

"Huh? What do you mean?" Snap scratched his head.

Herbert pointed his claw down the Pacific Coast Highway. "There, sir! I worked all night with my crew so it would be perfect this morning."

Turtle Town: The Inner Puka

"Your crew?" Snap looked in the direction of Herbert's claw to find his picture spread across his very own billboard.

"Congratulations Snap Shell! Turtle Town's First Box Shell Surfing Champion!"

"Beautiful, no?" Herbert asked, praising himself. He clapped his claws together, and Star hopped up onto Snap's shell.

"You two aren't so bad," Snap said. He knelt down to tap Herbert on the shell, which only knocked his goggles off his face. Star hopped off his back, found his customary place on Herbert's shell, and went to work nibbling as usual.

Snap took a closer look at the sign. "Wait! Herb! Is that you on the top of my surfboard?"

"Precisely. Doesn't my shell look superb?"

"Wait, Star, too? And with his coffee? Seriously?"

"You don't expect me to leave little Star out, do you?"

"But how did you get up there?"

"Photoshop, *monsieur*. Photoshop. Cut and paste is such a handy application."

"You photoshopped yourself and Star on the top of my surfboard?"

Star shrugged his shoulders.

"You're really something, Herb," Snap said. "And I don't care what anyone says, French crab or no French crab, you're one awesome Hermit Crab, dude."

"Oh," Herbert chuckled. "It's nothing, sir. I was doing you a favor."

"By putting yourself on my billboard?"

"It's all about who you know, *monsieur*. Networking, networking, networking."

"Yeah, Herb. It's all about you, alright."

About the Author

Melissa M. Williams has been writing stories since the age of eight years old. Many of her stories were inspired by real-life experiences with her reptile pets she owned while growing up in Houston, Texas. Melissa started her writing career while pursuing a Master's degree in professional counseling. During graduate school, she began substitute teaching for third and fourth grade classes, which encouraged her to get the students involved in the creative writing process of her books. Melissa continues to connect to her young readers by visiting schools and speaking to students about her journey while giving hands on insight into the writing and publishing process. Melissa also hosts writing workshops, summer camps and book clubs for her readers through out the year. Melissa's other titles include books in the *Iggy the Iguana* Series.

Be sure to check the author's websites:
www.MelissaMwilliamsAuthor.com
www.TurtleTownBooks.com
www.IggytheIguana.com

Acknowledgements

The writing of this book has been such an illuminating experience, as it has brought me to know so many incredible people and experience cultures outside of my own. I must first thank my Lord and Savior for the ability to develop gifts of childhood and use them to give back a creative part of myself to children and readers. I want to thank all of the kids whom I have been given the opportunity to visit over the years. It is their authentic energy that drives my stories. I would like to thank my parents for always encouraging art and imagination at a very young age and their continual support. I truly believe that we must encourage our youth to strive to fulfill their goals and dreams.

This book would not be where it is today, without the work and support of the LongTale Publishing team. I would like to thank my illustrator, Kelley Stengele, who has been there since day one, during the creation and development of the Iggy series. I am such a fan of your work and talent. Sharon Wyatt, my editor and graphic designer, you have been such a foundation to my projects,

Turtle Town: The Inner Puka

and I truly value your work across every venture we have encountered. Bobby Ozuna, your work as a story analyst from day one has challenged my writing and has taken this story to a new level. I would like to thank my extra eyes for always being there to watch over my work, Michele Williams and Allison Johnson. I can always count on both of you to be my first stage of support. Thank you to the team at TLC Graphics, Tamara and Tom Dever and my cover/interior designer, Monica Thomas. It has been such a blessing to work with all of you, and not just because we have so much fun, but your style and talent has put me at ease during this project. I'm so thankful you all have been brought into my life.

As I moved forward on the writing of this spin off to the Iggy the Iguana series, I took on the adventure of researching and experiencing the world of surfing, sea turtles and the West Coast culture. Many amazing mentors so graciously took me under their wing, offering their wisdom, their ears and eyes, and even their homes as I lived out life in California during a portion of the writing of this book. D.J. Fuller, Justin Jackson, Tim Collins, and my Alta roommates and San Diego friends, thank you for your generosity, friendship and resources during my exciting adventures on the West Coast. Ryan Gambrell, I can't thank you enough for taking me on my first surf out in Cardiff Beach and watching over my attempt to write about surf culture as an outsider looking in. You've guided an aspect of this story that could have only been done by someone of your veracity. A huge thank you goes out to Jake Marshall and the Marshall Family for your support during my year of surf research in California. Thank you Jake, for sharing your "Save Trestles" speech (pgs. 184–186) with me and allowing me and my character, Snap Shell, to use

Acknowledgments

some of your amazing words in an effort to bring awareness to that special surf location.

The opportunity to work with people from the California region has made the writing of this story so authentic and real. I would like to thank everyone from the San Diego Turtle and Tortoise Society for sharing valuable information with me and inviting me to be a part of your group. Your dedication to the awareness of these great species is so valuable to our world. Thank you to Jim Mayfield and Hannah Mayfield at Sub Sea Systems for sharing your mascot, Trekker, with the Turtle Town Series. Since our first meeting, I have only been more encouraged to be a part of the wonderful opportunities your organization provides to children and families across the globe. It was so much fun to give life and character to a real product started in California.

www.sea-trek.com

(left to right) Morgan Mayer, Shannon Kummer, Melissa Williams, and Logan Hibbeler.

Special Acknowledgements

It is my great pleasure to give a special thank you to my Turtle Town Character Development critique group, Logan Hibbeler, Shannon Kummer, and Morgan Mayer. After entering a contest during one of my creative writing summer camps in 2009, I had the privilege of choosing three talented students to develop a character for my next book. Our group came up with the dynamic duo, Herbert and his sidekick, Star. These creative writers have been a part of the creation process since the beginning. I have enjoyed our evenings developing ideas, and I value your thorough input as you participated in the brainstorming stages all the way to publication. I am so proud of all three of you and your writing accomplishments at such a young age.

Morgan is a 7th grader in the Cypress Fairbanks Independent School District and would like to be a veterinarian and animal conservationist when she grows up. Morgan is an avid reader and loves to write. Morgan decided Herbert would be a French crab with a one-of-a-kind attitude!

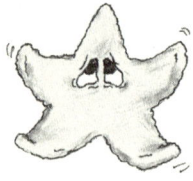

Shannon is a 7th grader in the Cypress Fairbanks Independent School District and would like to be a writer and director when she grows up. Shannon enjoys Taekwondo, acting, and reading. Shannon gave Herbert a pair of prescription goggles to add to his character!

Logan is a 6th grader in the Cypress Fairbanks Independent School District and would like to be a veterinarian when he grows up. He enjoys playing baseball, writing, and playing the guitar. Logan decided that Star would be a coffee-drinking starfish!

The Real Wrinklebutt

The character, "Wrinklebutt," was inspired by a real-life Eastern Pacific green sea turtle that has been known to visit the San Diego Bay. She was identified by M. Stinson in the 1970's and was named Wrinklebutt due to the deformity of her back shell, which makes her easily identifiable. Researchers have been studying and tracking her ever since. Researcher Dr. Jeff Seminoff, who is the leader of the Marine Turtle Ecology Assessment Program, shared with me that the last time the turtle was found was back in 2008, and she recorded to be 540 lbs. "She is the largest green turtle ever recorded in the eastern Pacific Ocean," states Dr. Seminoff. "She's been equipped with numerous transmitters over the years and we've been able to learn lots from her movements." He also shared that Wrinklebutt spends most of her time in the extreme south San Diego Bay and her diet consists of eelgrass (Zostera marina) and invertebrates.

Hi, Everyone!

Get your very own Snap Shell and Iggy books and merchandise. Just visit our web sites to see what's new and place your order today!

www.TurtleTownBooks.com
or www.IggytheIguana.com

Other books by Melissa Williams and featuring Iggy, Snap Shell, and their friends.

Iggy the Iguana
Book 1 of the Iggy the Iguana Series
ISBN 978-0-9818054-0-5 (pbk) $9.99

Summer League
Book 2 of the Iggy the Iguana Series
ISBN 978-0-9818054-2-9 (pbk) $9.99

All Books are also available at BarnesandNoble.com and Amazon.com.

For information about author school visits, creative writing workshops, and public speaking requests, e-mail melissa@longtalepublishing.com